The DOUBLE DIAMOND TRIANGLE SAGA™

Part 6

# CONSPIRACY

J. Robert King

# CONSPIRACY
©1998 TSR, Inc.
All Rights Reserved.

All characters in this book are fictitious. Any resemblance to actual persons, living or dead, is purely coincidental.

This book is protected under the copyright laws of the United States of America. Any reproduction or other unauthorized use of the material or artwork contained herein is prohibited without the express written permission of TSR, Inc.

Distributed to the book trade in the United States by Random House, Inc. and in Canada by Random House of Canada Ltd. Distributed to the hobby, toy, and comic trade in the United States and Canada by regional distributors. Distributed worldwide by Wizards of the Coast, Inc. and regional distributors.

Cover art by Heather LeMay.

FORGOTTEN REALMS and the TSR logo are registered trademarks owned by TSR, Inc. DOUBLE DIAMOND TRIANGLE SAGA is a trademark owned by TSR, Inc.

All TSR characters, character names, and the distinctive likenesses thereof are trademarks owned by TSR, Inc.

TSR, Inc. is a subsidiary of Wizards of the Coast, Inc.

First Printing: April 1998
Printed in the United States of America.
Library of Congress Catalog Card Number: 96-90569

9 8 7 6 5 4 3 2 1

8639XXX1501

ISBN: 0-7869-0869-6

| U.S., CANADA, ASIA, PACIFIC, & LATIN AMERICA | EUROPEAN HEADQUARTERS |
|---|---|
| Wizards of the Coast, Inc. | Wizards of the Coast, Belgium |
| P.O. Box 707 | P.B. 34 |
| Renton, WA 98057-0707 | 2300 Turnhout |
| +1-206-624-0933 | Belgium |
| | +32-14-44-30-44 |

Visit our website at **www.tsr.com**

Kern and Miltiades turned toward the sound, toward the coming of Tyr in glory. What they saw was not Tyr, though, but his enormous, bleeding apotheosis.

Aetheric III dragged himself up from the broken dome of his palace. His hands seized and smashed turrets. His tentacles coiled and recoiled in slug paths of steaming slime. His throat, so long filled with poison, roared.

*Doegan, behold your god!*

## The DOUBLE DIAMOND TRIANGLE SAGA™

### THE ABDUCTION
J. Robert King

### THE PALADINS
James M. Ward & David Wise

### THE MERCENARIES
Ed Greenwood

### ERRAND OF MERCY
Roger E. Moore

### AN OPPORTUNITY FOR PROFIT
Dave Gross

### CONSPIRACY
J. Robert King

### UNEASY ALLIANCES
David Cook with Peter Archer

### EASY BETRAYALS
Richard Baker

### THE DIAMOND
J. Robert King & Ed Greenwood

**To Elaine Cunningham,
first among
Those Who Harp**

### Prelude

# *Conceit*

I'm mesmerized by you.

I lie upon this rough-hewn bed and watch you. My head is pillowed on big dry sponges, piled against a coral headboard. You're the only fine thing in this room.

Lord Garkim has said that this bedchamber, like all of the mage-king's lower palace, was once part of a sea cave. The stone walls here were carved out by generations of tides. Even the brown blankets I lie upon come from the ocean, woven from seaweed. The mattress is just a net of kelp. I feel like a netted fish.

But you, you make me feel like a king. You don't come from this barbarous place. You're not rough, reeking of brine. You're smooth and fine, lithe and magical. You move from the bed to the limestone doorknob and then back with a round-hipped dance. Your golden strands tickle along my chest as I gather you in.

"Let's have another go," I whisper to you.

Listen to me, speaking as if you were Aleena Paladinstar. But how could I compare her to you? You're only a bit of rope. Golden, yes, but still, you're rope.

You seem eager to fly again.

I twirl your looped head once more before releasing you. Your smooth sinew snakes to my idle day pack, where the broken buckle protrudes. You snap down to grasp it. Your line goes taut.

You're so nimble, so precise, my golden lasso. You can lay hold of a fly's wing without brushing its leg. You can catch whatever I desire within fifty feet, no matter how large or small. You go out like a golden messenger. You leap from my hand and cross this room to grasp that clamshell coat peg or that nautilus lantern or that whalebone pitcher.

I send you coiling out again. You seize the doorknob. I flick you free, careful not to open the door; there are paladins out there. Real paladins. Once I was only too eager for their company. Now, I dread it.

I don't want to be like them—stiff, loud, indelicate. I want to be like you, my golden lariat. I want to be facile and silent, lithe and quick, strong but smooth and sleek and golden. I don't want to be like Miltiades or Kern, but like Piergeiron Paladinson. He doesn't pray for truth. He goes out and wrestles it. That's what I want. I want to be like you, golden lariat, going out to grasp whatever I seek.

I flip my wrist. You lightly grip the bed knob, carved from driftwood. I tug, but this time you are snagged, so tight is your hold. I sit up and pry you loose. You leap to coil into my open hand.

"Let's have another go."

## Chapter 1

## *Convergence*

*We heard and saw it all.*

*Perhaps in our madness, we have forgotten some of the minutia, but we are like the sea. Only truth survives our ceaseless churning; we melt falsity into silt.*

*We remember truth. We remember how the catastrophes of Doegan were set into motion. And when. And by whom. We were there. We were everywhere. We heard and saw it all.*

*The catastrophes were triggered one fine morning within our own walls. . . .*

The Fountain of the Kraken sprayed tentacles of

briny mist into the air. Ocean breezes caught the questing arms of fog and spread them low and flat over the Plaza of the Mage-King. From there, the mists sifted past slums before sliding through the teeth of the outer wall. The fog scintillated for a moment, transfixed on slaying wards, and then moved on, across a scoured plain of salted ground and into the arid forest beyond. What happened to the mist next, only trees and fiends could have told.

Trees, fiends, and a haggard crew of pirates. A short while ago, they had entered the city of Eldrinpar, capital of Doegan. The claw slashes carved across their arms, chests, and legs told that they had come by way of the fiend-filled forest. No one came through that death trap. And what were pirates doing so far away from ship and sea?

Their leader was short, dark-haired, and olive-skinned. He had muscles like silken cords and eyes keen as razors. He was no pirate. This one preferred dark caves to the bright sea. He was as comfortable on land as any wolf. Like a wolf, his chief weapons were concealed, small and deadly. He wore a sword, but not a swaggering cutlass like those of his companions. They knew him as Belmer, though he knew himself by another name—one he had buried deeply.

His companions were the real pirates. They were swarthy locals from Doegan, Edenvale, and Ulgarth. They stepped hard on their heels and lingered too long on tiptoes, their legs accustomed to rolling decks instead of dead ground. The cut of their jerkins showed tailoring. No mere seaman could afford this expense. A privateer might—especially if he had new gold in need of being hastily spent. Pirates, yes: their eyes were as cold and calm as ball lightning.

The woman was obviously an accomplished fighter. Pirate ships are not virgin vaults. To survive, free, with a face and body like hers, she was more than able to defend herself. Her tan visage was flawless, set with sapphire eyes and an even row of gleaming teeth, forming a comely smile.

Sharessa "the Shadow" Stagwood, or Shar.

What of the rest? There was a moon-faced sharper with deft hands. He could slay as surely with cards as with blades. He aided a staggering young man, blind and bloodied. Behind these two came a seaman whose red jags of hair and beard blended smoothly with the orange scars lining his face. Then a dwarf, whose ears and nose jingled with electrum rings. His eyes were fixed in a wary, haunted stare. Last in the company was a tired sea captain, his large frame compromised by a gut of rotten wood. He had the look of a plague ship. The bilge rats had risen up to take possession of him, and he smelled of death.

The olive-faced man led his tattered party to the long, curving edge of the great fountain. There, one by one, they knelt, scooped up water, and laved away mud, grit, blood, and exhaustion. The fountain flowed with salt water. In it, they washed. They knelt at the cool stone rim as if at an altar stone, and washed as if with holy water. Released from a long ordeal, they laughed and sported in the fountain's basin until called to order by their leader.

The fountain was, indeed, an altar. The statue of a god stood in its center: a man wrestling a great kraken. His anguished face, frozen in chiseled marble, had eyes bored deep into his skull. In one mighty hand, he gripped a constricting tentacle. In the other, he held a trident, thrust down among more octopus arms. The jetting sprays of water showed how the battle of these colossi churned the oceans of the world.

So grand was this tableaux that the mercenaries could not see their opponents.

The men approaching on the other side were in every way the pirates' opposites. In place of tattered rags, most wore polished armor that glared silver and gold in the sun. Instead of staggering, they marched. Instead of bowing to the statue, the warriors turned their backs. One even sat down on the fountain rail, as though it were a mere bench. Another produced a golden lasso and sent its silent loop whirring up to snag one of the marble tentacles.

Paladins. Their glamorous armor, ridiculous in this brutal heat, meant they were paladins, madmen, or both.

Their leader was larger than life, with thick black hair streaked with gray, a granite jaw, silver armor, and a cold, unyielding demeanor. His eyes narrowed, and his gaze swept the adobe buildings ringing the plaza. There was evil here, and he could sense it. His hand strayed to the warhammer at his side.

In the shadow of the silver warrior stood a younger man, garbed in gold. His mail shimmered across a large heart. His eyes watched his mentor. He sensed the man's unease and also reached for his hammer.

These two were flanked by three others. The first was a silver-haired warrior with leather armor and a quarterstaff. Beside him was the young man who sat on the fountain edge. He had blond curls and a jaunty sword. Last of all was a lightly armored youth, absently flinging his golden lasso.

The silver paladin gestured to the others. "Check this plaza. Report any strange signs, especially symbols of Tyr perverted by fanatics of the Fallen Temple. Once we find the Fallen Temple, we will find Lady Eidola. As true believers, we must rescue not only the lady, but also the worship of Tyr in this savage land."

The others nodded, all except the youth. His lasso was snagged about the granite head of the wrestling god.

The golden paladin said to his leader, "Miltiades, might I suggest we go in pairs, ready for ambush?"

"Excellent, Kern. You come with me, but give your pendant to Trandon. Your antimagic aura may well be preventing the pendant from sensing Lady Eidola."

Kern's sweating, sunburned face colored more deeply. He lifted the jeweled pendant from his neck and handed it to the leather-armored man. "You're right, of course. It was only my pride that made me hold on to it."

"We'll patrol this side of the plaza." Miltiades gestured to the seated fighter and said, "Jacob, you and Trandon check out the other side." Miltiades turned toward the youth with the lasso. "And, Noph, get that rope off the statue before the mage-king's men haul you away."

Noph peered along the dripping length of his rope. He gave it two more flips, shaking saltwater from it. The lasso did not come loose. Noph sighed and stepped over the stony rim, into the pool. Up to his knees in seawater, he visibly shivered.

Shaking his head, Miltiades said, "Let's go."

*The paladins and pirates were destined to meet, as fresh water flows ever into the salty sea. But they need not have clashed so soon, or so violently. We had hoped, in fact, to keep them separate, to use them both. The paladins were useful for fighting our deadliest foes—the terrorists who called themselves the Fallen Temple. The pirates, on the other hand—we could smell their greed. They had come for riches and glory. They would be easy to manipulate. Before the tenday was done, they would be fighting for Doegan, too.*

*But it was not to be. The gods had placed a catalyst among them. A traitor. We could smell him. Traitors always smell of decay.*

*Among the pirates was a weak-bellied sea captain. He had lost his ship and, with it, his last scraps of courage and dignity. All that remained to drive him were despair, rage, and shame, the humors of betrayal.*

*Captain Jander Turbalt—let history dote on the traitor's name—had sold his companions even before he shuffled casually toward Kern and Miltiades and betrayed his leader.*

"Excuse me, sirs, but you appear to be on official business," Turbalt said, grovelling ostentatiously.

"We are conducting an investigation into the Fallen Temple with the sanction of the mage-king," answered Kern.

"Perfect," said Turbalt. He wrung his hands in nervous anticipation. "Do not be obvious in looking, sirs, but the scrofulous band of pirates behind me have held me captive for the last weeks. They kidnapped me aboard my own ship, forced me to sail into the worst of storms, and destroyed my *Morning Bird* right out from under me. They've since dragged me across desert and dale, through fiend dens and icy streams. It is only by the good grace of the gods and my own courage—not to boast of it, though—that I have lived long enough to tell you."

*These were, perhaps, not the actual words the coward spoke. We do not remember; so much has happened since. The captain may have merely identified his leader, Belmer, as an illegal immigrant. Or he may have spoken Belmer's true name; we do not recall. The words are lost, but not the traitor's name or his fate.*

"Blessed hammer of Tyr," Kern remarked. He gazed past the man, and so did not see the captain's ingenuous look. "Look who that man is, there in front."

"Hold there," Miltiades called out toward the little man. The paladin drew his warhammer and marched toward the pirates. "We would speak with you." Kern followed likewise, and called the others.

The olive-skinned man smiled falsely. "Perhaps later. We have pressing business in another part of the city."

The silver paladin spoke in a voice of command. "I said hold. I am Miltiades of Tyr, and I speak with the authority of Justice. I wish to know what you are doing in Doegan—why the Sword Coast's most notorious assassin has come to the Utter East! Tell us, why have you come here, Artemis Entreri?"

Without awaiting a reply, Miltiades and Kern closed upon the stunned man and his party of pirates. Silver-haired Trandon and young Jacob also charged inward. Only Noph Nesher did not attack, busy climbing to the top of the fountain to free his lasso.

The rotten-bellied captain, meanwhile, made to slink away.

Artemis Entreri drew a small, deadly blade from concealment and flung it through the fountain's mist. The steel flashed for a breath before it buried itself in Captain Jander Turbalt's head. The sound was like a snake biting into an egg. The man's limbs went limp, though he remained upright, as if the dagger pinned him to the sky. Then he dropped.

He flopped into the base of the fountain. Tentacles of gore reached out from his pulpy head, toward the wrestling god, as though in mockery.

The pirates rallied to Entreri—all but one, the blind young man Ingrar. He drew his blade and shouted, " 'Ware! Paladins!"

*Could he smell paladins?—old armor scrubbed and waxed to shine hot beneath a cruel sun? Could he hear paladins?—voices of virtue in a world of vice? Somehow, he knew what and who they were. We marked this young man, Ingrar. He had gained a unique blessing. No longer could his eyes fool him. No longer was he the victim of illusions—double images and double walkers. The windows of his higher self were shuttered; the windows of his lower self, his animal self, were flung wide.*

Black-haired Miltiades roared a holy vow and brought his warhammer singing down at Entreri's upraised sword. The massive hammer cracked off to one side and swung down by the paladin's hip.

Entreri's blade had no sooner deflected that attack than its tip danced in to jab beneath the warrior's breastplate. The tongue of steel tasted blood.

Miltiades pried it away with the head of his hammer and staggered back to take the measure of his foe.

In that moment's confrontation, just before the other fighters met in skirls of steel, Entreri and Miltiades saw each other truly.

It was as though these two men had been fashioned as eternal champions of opposite gods, and these two champions had battled their way across hilltop, threshold, and whitecap, through hundreds of pages of history, to converge at this spot beside this fountain. The statue at its center was, after all, a stone avatar of them, of their struggle against each other, the figure of a man wrestling the ineffable and inescapable unknown. All that remained was to determine which of them—Miltiades or Entreri—was the striving human hero and which the grasping and implacable monster.

The others converged.

The young golden warrior Kern hurled his hammer down at the onrushing head of the pirate woman, Sharessa. She had the foresight not to get beneath the maul. Kern overbalanced himself, a true idealist, and tumbled head over heels past Sharessa.

She stepped out of his way and helped him along, whacking the flat of her cutlass against his unarmored rump. She flipped her dark hair back over her slender shoulders and jested, "Find some hay, Sir Knight, and I'll roll you in that, too."

Kern, unamused, got up and advanced. "I can't decide whether you're worse off for having truck with this vicious scoundrel," he waved his hammer toward Entreri, "or he for having truck with you." With that, the golden warrior lunged. His hammer grazed Sharessa's narrow belly as she leapt back.

"Such language," the pirate laughed, "and from a

paladin. If you aren't careful with that hammer of yours, I'll end up having truck with you!" She followed her comment with a suggestively lifted eyebrow and a wickedly thrust cutlass.

The paladin had overcome his zeal and shame. His hammer struck away the sword, and he stepped close enough to plant an elbow guard in the woman's side. It was Sharessa's turn to roll away, grunting.

Kern stalked after her. "Surrender to me and quit your dealings with this assassin!"

Sharessa leapt lightly to her feet and drove the golden warrior back with a hail of blows. "Jealous, are we?"

Between the two, Miltiades suddenly appeared. He barged backward, propelled to the fountain's edge by Entreri, who followed hard behind. Miltiades's face was red and running with sweat. It dripped miserably into his steaming armor. He groaned with each swing of his hammer, but so far had only grazed his opponent.

Entreri sweated too, though in an even sheen of tiny droplets. The veins in his temples bulged with exertion. His sword darted and fluttered like a bird. All the while, his head remained still, his expression calm, his eyes intent.

Miltiades caught his balance at the low brink of the fountain. He hurled out a wide swing of his hammer and halted Entreri's advance.

The small man danced inward, despite the paladin's swings. He was about to jab for an exposed rib when a roar broke the din of battle. The sound ended in a crackle and thud. The fight paused, and the fighters saw.

The pirate named Anvil had once had a scarred face, but it was gone. In its place was the bloody end of a two-handed sword, whose hilt was even then held in the grip of the young, blond paladin, Jacob.

As the headless body collapsed, the bristle-bearded

dwarf, Rings, furiously attacked the killer. The stout pirate jabbed inward. Jacob clutched the bleeding wound and crumpled, replaced in turn by the leather-clad paladin. Trandon landed a solid whump of his quarterstaff on the dwarf's shoulder. Rings proved heartier than previous fighters, whirling with an oath and striking back.

*Three down already—a traitor, a veteran, and a young paladin. We were impressed. We were entertained. We were not yet fearful, though we should have been. For every stranger that fell in that battle, a thousand of our people would die.*

Miltiades and Entreri hammered and jabbed their way around the fountain; Kern and Sharessa engaged in amorous swordplay; Trandon and Rings traded blow for blow; blind Ingrar clutched the fountain rail while waving his sword; Jacob bled quietly; Belgin breathed raggedly; the bodies of Anvil and Captain Jander Turbalt cooled in death.

Noph, meanwhile, had at last surmounted the slippery, roaring fountain. Clinging with one hand to an up-flung tentacle, he reached the statue's neck and began lifting the lasso free. Until now the spraying water had masked the shouts and hidden the glint of swords. His lasso came loose and coiled in his hand.

But what to do?

The lasso. It did not err. It caught anything he desired. He could rope the leader of the brigands.

Noph flung the rope up. It whistled coyly overhead. The golden loop widened above the fountain. White spray shot past it as it grew. One more circle, and Noph would fling the lariat to snare the leader of the cutthroats and save the day!

Unless . . . unless *she* were their leader.

He gaped at her. The pirate woman moved with the sinuous seduction of a serpent. Mystery beyond comprehension. Noph had never seen so vibrant a creature.

Every part of her was tightly and perfectly arranged. Curves appeared where they should, and flat spots in their places, too. She was muscular and soft in divine proportions. She could, from any visible distance, make a young man faint.

Noph almost obliged. He felt himself sliding back along the tentacle. His vision closed to a dark tunnel whose terminus was the deadly beauty. Noph lurched, catching himself. Blood dissolved the shadows at the edges of his sight.

During his blackout, the lasso had flown.

His shaky gaze traced along the now-taut line. The cutthroat leader struggled impotently at the end of the golden lasso. So, too, did Miltiades. Noph had snared both.

*It was the end of the convergence. The fighting faltered and stopped. The fighters gazed at their captured commanders. Noph shivered atop our effigy.*

*It was the end of the convergence, and the beginning of the end for Doegan.*

*We heard and saw it all.*

## Chapter 2

## *Confession*

"You worthless, whining whelp! You spoiled, slow-witted stripling. I knew you would be trouble from the moment I laid eyes on your overstuffed pack bulging over your understuffed brain! And trouble is all you have been this entire journey!"

The tirade came from Miltiades, who struggled in the embrace of Entreri, both of whom were squeezed near suffocation by Noph's golden lasso. The fight was over. Still, the bloodstained leaders tried to continue it. The best they could do was strike each other lightly in the back of the head.

"So what if you foiled an assassination plot? So what if you rounded up the conspirators in Waterdeep? So what if you slew a golem creature in our chambers? Lady Eidola is still kidnapped. With you along, I doubt she will ever be rescued!" Miltiades shouted, his voice echoing through the plaza.

The others—paladins and pirates—stood side-by-side and gaped at the furious warrior.

Noph, ignoring the insults, shouted to the leader of the cutthroats, "Who are you?"

The little man looked up. Though his eyes were defiant, his mouth produced the words, "I am Artemis Entreri, master assassin, and bane of the Sword Coast"

Noph gulped.

The pirates gaped in astonishment.

The paladins tightened holds on their weapons.

Only Kern, Miltiades, and Entreri seemed unsurprised.

"Why is an assassin of the north stirring up trouble here in the Utter East?"

With the same grudging glare, Entreri spoke again. His lips moved slowly, distorting the words. "I have come to find Eidola Neverwinter—kin of Boarskyr and bride of Piergeiron Paladinson—come to find her and kill her."

That news shocked even Kern and Miltiades.

"Release me, imbecile boy," Miltiades suggested. "I must fight this man to the death, here and now!"

"Wait," called Trandon. "Noph, I suspect your lasso does more than bind. It has our two leaders under some sort of enchantment. They seem incapable of hiding the truth from us. Noph, don't release them until the assassin tells us all."

Noph nodded seriously, tightening his grip.

Trandon approached the roped pair. His quarterstaff thumped dully against the cobbles as he leaned on it, wizardlike. "Tell us, Artemis Entreri, who hired you?"

"I do not know," the assassin replied, a look of triumph

in his eyes. "I know only that the masked figure claimed to be a Lord of Waterdeep, a friend of Piergeiron's—and that he paid a handsome advance for the work."

Trandon nodded. "Why would a friend of Piergeiron's want the Open Lord's bride to be slain?"

Entreri's face clenched, pale with effort, but the magical power of the lasso was inexorable. "He said she was an agent of the Unseen."

Miltiades stiffened. He stared fiercely into the assassin's eyes. "The Unseen? Eidola consorting with tentacled horrors and black-hearted monsters? Impossible!"

"Yet that is what my employer said," replied Entreri.

"And you were a fool to believe him. If Eidola worked for the Unseen, she could have slain Piergeiron long ago. What was she waiting for?"

"The wedding," Noph blurted. The others looked up at him, and he sheepishly continued. "She could do more harm to Waterdeep as Lady Paladinson than as a mere assassin, couldn't she? She could control everything through him. After the trade pact, her reach would extend all the way to Kara-Tur."

Noph had not known what he was going to say until the words tumbled out, but they seemed right. The trade pact. That's what this whole nasty business came down to. Half the people in Waterdeep wanted to prevent it and the other half to control it. But what would anyone in the Utter East care about an overland route that didn't pass within a thousand miles of . . . ?

Again, a flash of insight. These tiny countries needed trade, they needed mercenaries to fight their battles, they needed wealth and power. All of it could be given them by a route that was half land and half sea. Ships would dock right here, in this steamy seaport, and their loads would be transferred to elephants for the overland leg. Returning caravans would stop in Eldrinpar to transfer their cargoes to ships. Doegan could tax items going and coming.

That was why Eidola had been kidnapped, Noph thought bitterly. For cash. Cold hard cash.

While Noph ruminated, Trandon continued to question the assassin. But he learned nothing more of the man's mission or his employer. The only further fact that emerged was that Entreri had hired the pirates, straggling survivors of a shipwreck, for a chest of gold coins apiece.

"What if your employer is no friend of Piergeiron's?" Noph broke in. "What if Eidola is an innocent woman, not an agent of evil?"

"I don't care about whom I kill or whom I kill for. The only thing I care about is whether I get paid. If I don't, whom I kill and whom I kill for become the same person."

"Let me out of this Tyr-blasted rope, Noph," Miltiades groused, "before your clumsiness kills me as it killed Harloon!"

Noph winced. For a moment the world around him disappeared. The tan cobbles softened and melted to form a face—the face of Harloon, whose life had bought Noph from death, and whose death had granted him the golden lasso he now held.

Except that the rope looked red. Everything suddenly looked red. The white sprays of water had turned to bloody crimson.

Noph shivered, blinking, but the stain remained. He looked down at the sanguine fountain. Captain Jander Turbalt's body bobbed in the water, one of Entreri's daggers jutting from his head.

I betrayed Harloon, Noph thought bitterly. He stared at the captain's gushing head. That's who I am, right there. A traitor.

"Let me loose, you immature imbecile!" Miltiades demanded. "How can I baby-sit you if you've got me all tied up?"

He sounds just like Father, Noph thought angrily. I traveled half the world to escape my father, but he's still here. This preening, self-important, unappreciative paladin has become my father. Noph couldn't bear the thought of spending another moment with him, and his shoulders stiffened in sudden resolve.

"I'll let you both go on one condition," he said. He climbed steadily down the bloody statue. "That you, Miltiades, let Master Entreri and his crew slip away with their wounded and dead into the city."

"What?" Miltiades demanded of Noph. "You would let these black-hearted brigands go, though you know they seek to kill the very lady you are sworn to rescue?"

As Noph climbed down the slippery slope, he said, "That was your oath, not mine." He reached the bloody pool at the base of the fountain, and sloshed purposefully through it, drawing the rope tight all the while. "Besides, as you said, you'd probably never rescue her with me along."

Miltiades's eyes shown as with battle fury. "You are quitting our band? How dare you? You will not survive an hour alone in this city!"

An arm was on Noph's shoulders, a slender and strong arm, and he was whirled forcefully around into a hot embrace. The she-pirate Shar kissed him long and full on the lips. She drew her head back, staring with promise in her eyes and laughing scornfully. "You may not survive the hour, my luscious little lad, but I've got arms you can die in." She tossed a grin toward the pair of roped leaders, both of whom looked equally mortified. "The kid's coming with me. Call him a spoiled little spoil of war. And don't get too jealous, Entreri. He just saved your skin. I'm simply returning the favor." She bent closer to the dark little man and hissed so only he could hear, "You've kept enough secrets from us. Perhaps now I'll start making some secrets of my own." She swung her eyes back to the boy and gave him a delicious smile.

Noph turned his hurt gaze away from his erstwhile mentor and toward the brazen, voluptuous she-pirate. "I'm one of you, now."

The paladin's eyes strayed to the tatter-clothed and sensuous woman. "Agreed. Go with them. You deserve each other. As for you, Entreri, I will slay you another time."

\* \* \* \* \*

Into the bloodstained Plaza of the Mage-King came the most feared man in Eldrinpar, followed by forty of his picked men.

Perhaps a year ago, Ikavi Garkim would have brought only twenty men, but now, every last soldier of Doegan's native forces was weak with the Gray Malaise. The city's priests had failed to find a cure, and those infected grew slowly, agonizingly worse. Already hundreds of civilians had died from it, and the malaise was beginning to cripple the army.

Even Garkim, King Aetheric's right-hand man, felt the prickling itch beneath his collar, the sluggishness of his feet, and the chronic headaches. He would not coddle himself, though. A telepath, a matchless warrior, and a Mar, Garkim held Eldrinpar together. Morning sunlight shone from his keen eyes and black hair, drawn back in a tight skein. He looked anything but ill. He cut a commanding figure, bearing the full authority of his master—and his master's bloodforge.

Garkim halted his weary troops, and he studied the scene.

Blood was everywhere. The statue of Aetheric—which peasants thought to be merely a man wrestling a kraken—was painted in blood. Who had died here, and why? The Mar had reported a riot among outlanders, but surely Miltiades and his paladins would not riot, and what other outlanders had come to Eldrinpar since the siege of the fiends?

"Fan out. Search the surrounding hovels," Garkim commanded his troops, dressed in the light leather armor of battle. He flung his arm out, pointing at the bloodstains. The sun glared like lightning from the lining of his cloak. "There and there. Find out what happened to the bodies."

As his soldiers complied, images flooded into Garkim's mind . . . a man as small and sharp as a stiletto . . . another as huge and powerful as a two-handed sword . . . a woman of mystery . . . a disguised mage . . . a young man with a heart the size of Faerûn . . .

Noph. The boy. So, Miltiades and his paladins *had* been here, *had* fought someone. Garkim could glimpse seafarers . . . privateers. But who led them? Ah, it was that small stiletto of a man, with a mind as poisonous as any Garkim had ever encountered. The presence of that mind in his own only intensified his migraine. What lay within the man's thoughts was too dark, too violent to be easily perceived. But there was something here of murder—no, of assassination. Not the mage-king, but a lady of high station. Eidola. The woman for whom the paladins were searching. And there was something else—something about the heart of Doegan. . . .

That was all. Garkim could stand no more. His head felt as though it were splitting beneath a cording wedge.

*"Do not bother to question witnesses."*

The voice that spoke was an unmistakable one, like the basso rumble of a sounding whale or the depthless churning of the sea. Usually Aetheric III spoke directly into Garkim's mind; this time, the Thorass words came from outside, from nearby.

*"We heard and saw it all."*

Garkim spun, just in time to see the lips of the bloody statue close. He glared up at the stone figure, utterly still above him. Another of Aetheric's damned golems. The king could see through thousands of eyes in this city.

As if in confirmation, the statue's lips opened again.

*"We heard and saw it all."*

## Chapter 3

## Contradiction

Sweating beneath the midday sun, Miltiades and his three companions marched down a roadway of glaring adobe and staring Mar. Other Ffolk who ventured into these slums might not venture out again, but these four were well armed, and clearly insane. That fact was obvious not just from their plate armor and sunburned faces, but also from the questions they asked:

*"Have you seen any false followers of the true god Tyr?"*

It was a nonsense question, though none of the Mar would tell them so. Instead, they merely shook their heads and averted their eyes.

Miltiades huffed irritably. He regretted everything that had happened today, everything since the fountain—the battle, the slain pirate, the stalemate, the truths he had told to young Noph. It seemed odd that he, a paladin, could regret uttering the truth, but he could not remember his words without wincing.

But worse than all these setbacks was the task that loomed before him: hunt down the terrorist core of the Fallen Temple and pry Eidola from their heretical grasp.

The Fallen Temple. The Fallen of Tyr. Miltiades could imagine no more onerous task than confronting the foul apostates of his own god.

Not just apostates. Violent revolutionaries, political terrorists . . . cannibals. Garkim had warned them of the depravities of those they sought. He had told even of following the stink of smoldering flesh to the house where he had been raised, to discover a band of cultists around a spitted and roasting foe. How could followers of Tyr—the one-handed, blind-eyed god of Justice—have fallen so far?

"What's this?" Kern asked. His pace slowed, and he sniffed dubiously at the air. There was a sickly-sweet stench on the wind. "Burning flesh?"

"Yes," Miltiades replied. He drew forth his hammer. "It smells like the pyres of Phlan, the burning grounds."

"Didn't Garkim say the worshipers of the Fallen Temple—?"

"Ate human flesh, yes," Miltiades said grimly. The words tangled chokingly in the rank breeze. "I had hoped we might convert some of these blasphemers, but what justice is there for those who eat the dead? Perhaps only that they, themselves, die."

Kern pointed toward a cluster of two-story adobe hovels ahead. Thin jags of black smoke rose from behind the lodgepole rafters. "There. It's coming from there."

Miltiades nodded and gestured to the other paladins to gather up beside him. "We go. Weapons out." He strode at an angry half-run toward the ragged black doorway of the nearest building.

Kern, Trandon, and Jacob followed.

The heat of exertion was stoked by that of fury. To impugn the holy name of Tyr was bad enough, but to do so with such despicable ceremonies as this? To flaunt all that was right and good by sinking teeth into a corpse and ...

The realization came to him out of the very wind, and it struck with all the horrible weight of truth. Eidola. That was why they had taken her. To parade her through some atrocious ceremony, slay her atop an altar desecrated with their sacrifices, and consume her. Cannibals often ate the brains, livers, and hearts of their victims, hoping to gain wisdom, strength, and courage. These cultists, though, sought not the vitality of one warrior woman, but of a whole city—of all Waterdeep.

What justice for monsters such as these?

Miltiades charged through the gaping doorway, into a small, dark, cluttered room, bulging with woven mats and crumpled sheets, chipped cups and a pitcher half-full of something red, a tangle of rope and a vacant chair. "Tyr's hammer! She was held captive here last night," Miltiades muttered to himself as he strode through the room. "Tied to that chair, and drained of her very blood, in that pitcher."

From a dark doorway at the back of the chamber came another whiff of burning flesh. The smoke brought with it a low chant—a multitude of Mar voices joined in a deep unison. The scissoring click of teeth and tongues made the song grate, ghastly and diabolical, in Miltiades's ears.

Even now, in the lot behind this house, the Fallen Temple is burning her to death, Miltiades thought.

He stomped through the dark doorway into another room, this one with a mean table lined with low candle stubs. He had no time to inspect the object—no doubt a sacrificial altar—for through a pair of double doors, he glimpsed the courtyard, and the scene of monstrous desecration in it.

Some twenty dark-robed Mar stood in a circle around a stack of wood, upon which lay Eidola, in silver breastplate and flowing gown. Her face, darkened by the sun of this hostile place, was twisted in an expression of agony, and her hands curled in tight fists to her chest. Her legs, too, were drawn up beneath the flowing gown, as if she had died in racking pain.

Yes, she was dead, for not a muscle moved on that pile of wood. She was dead, or soon would be. Already, the flames ringed her round in a wall five feet high.

With a righteous roar, Miltiades flung back the double doors and emerged at a run into the courtyard. He swung his hammer in an arc that would pulverize two of the robed heads and splatter them against a third. The wicked celebrants fell back before his onslaught. The silver hammerhead only grazed a shoulder, but that slight contact alone was enough to send the worshiper sprawling.

Not pausing to finish off this foe, Miltiades leapt through the searing wall of fire that surrounded Eidola. He landed beside her in the blazing inferno, snatched her from the smoldering pallet, and wrapped his vast arms around her. Then, his own tabard and cape blazing, Miltiades vaulted through the fire and landed in a crouch beyond. Ignoring the flash of his hair, singing away across his scalp, Miltiades gently laid Eidola down on a verge of grass. He then stood, flung off his burning livery, and hoisted his hammer.

Kern, Trandon, and Jacob had emerged behind him. With hammer, staff, and sword, they had corralled the cultists in a frightened mob at one corner of the courtyard.

Miltiades strode toward them and swung his smoking maul ominously overhead.

"Who is your master!" he roared. "I will slay only him. But if you conceal from me his whereabouts, I will slay each of you in turn!"

A small-framed Mar, eyes raging in his middle-aged face, said, "Who are you? What right have you to do this?"

"Are you the leader of these . . . these infidels?" Miltiades asked, leveling his hammer at the man.

"I am head of this household, and I demand by what right you—"

"By what right?" Miltiades shouted as he drew himself to his full height before the man. "By what right? By the right of justice. By the right of honor and decency. By the authority of Piergeiron Paladinson of Waterdeep and Emperor Aetheric III of Doegan—"

"These rulers give you the right to barge into our funeral service, break my nephew's shoulder with that hammer of yours, rip my mother from her pyre, and threaten to kill us all?" the man replied, incredulous.

Miltiades's lips drew up in a sneer, "It is too late for your lies. You have slain Lady Eidola of Neverwinter, and for that you will pay in blood."

"What? Slain whom?"

A staying hand fell upon Miltiades's shoulder, and he whirled in anger, almost striking Kern with his hammer. The golden paladin did not shy back, only saying softly, "Look. He's right. Look at the body. That woman is Mar. She's old. She's not Eidola."

Face red from sun and exertion and burns, Miltiades stared at the body he had rescued from the pyre. Kern was right. She was Mar, a withered crone. "B-But how do we know this is a funeral," Miltiades hissed to Kern, "and not a cannibalistic ritual?"

Kern's voice was barely a whisper. "There would have been nothing left of her to eat. Let's go, Miltiades. We need rest. We can search more tomorrow. We need rest."

"Yes," the silver knight said heavily. He took a staggering step away from the Mar, gaping behind him. "Yes. I'm weary to the bone."

"Wait. What of my family? What of my wounded nephew, and my dishonored mother?" the Mar man called after the retreating knights. "What justice is there for us? What justice for the Mar?"

## Chapter 4
## *Confabulation*

No longer in tatters, Artemis Entreri, Shar, her new plaything, Noph, and the band of pirates settled in beside the garden pool of a local tavern.

Prior to their arrival, they had "requisitioned" a loaded clothesline behind a noble estate. Now the whole crew was dressed in the fine, flowing clothes favored by the natives of Eldrinpar. After changing, they sought a safe tavern where they could rest and eat. The first two places, hung with huge signs and overflowing with patrons, were vetoed by Ingrar. He said they smelled metallic, like death.

They all had had enough death for one day.

The tavern where they ended up looked, on the outside, like nothing at all. Its walls were flaking adobe, its windows draped with tattered curtains. It seemed more a collection of slumping hovels than a safe house. Still, Ingrar swore by the aroma of the place—comfortable coolness beneath ragged eaves. He was right. Venturing through a vacant outer room, the company came to a fine establishment, patronized exclusively by elite Mar.

While any pub in the Heartlands would center around a hearth, this cafe centered on an open-air courtyard that held a tranquil pool. The eaves over the pool were high and broad, providing shade and secrecy from the eyes of flying things. The walls were more window than wall, letting restless sea winds shift among the beams.

The pool was a kind of urban oasis, edged in azure tile and surrounded by swaying palms and trailing vines. Tables were hidden among the dense growth so that patrons had a sense of seclusion. The secret cafe was, in a word, inviting.

The owner, at first, was not. The light-skinned pirates and white-skinned Noph made him very nervous. Ffolk rarely came to this secret spot, and never in the company of Mar. For some moments after their arrival, the owner flitted around like a catbird hosting cats. When his initial panic wore off, he decided to treat these guests like royalty. Dangerous royalty. They were seated at the best table, promised the finest ales and the fattest cuts of meat, and told it all was on the house. The pirates greedily accepted.

Seated in the cool shade of a gently breathing palm, the battle-torn company was finally at ease. As they drank the first round of thin, sharp-edged ale, they began to feel downright talkative. Noph, seated between voluptuous Shar and algid Entreri, was the most talkative of all.

"What was that fellow's name? The one with all the scars? The one we hid in the crate, dockside?"

The faces of the pirates grew grave.

Shar leaned heavily back in her seat and folded arms over her chest. A warm fragrance came from her and wafted around Noph. "His name was Anvil—well, really Jolloth Burbuck. He was a veteran of many battles. A stalwart seaman. A good friend."

The faces around the table were long. Even Entreri wore a tired look.

Noph ventured, "Then doesn't he deserve a decent burial?"

"Tonight," Shar said. Her eyes turned on Noph as though she were hurt by his insinuation. "We'll go back to the dock and bury him at sea." Her look hardened. "More important, we'll kill that Jacob fellow for him. Only then will he really rest."

"You know, when my best friend Harloon died—" Noph paused, biting his lip "—the paladins wanted to just leave him lying on the bank of the river, beside a dead ettin."

"Typical," snorted the dwarf, Rings. "They've no love for anybody. They're too busy being good."

"I'm glad to be rid of them," Noph said, lifting the sloshing dregs of his first-ever ale. The ruddy faces of the pirates around him warmed, and he took it as encouragement. "A bunch of primps, so worried they might sully a sleeve they never get around to being really noble."

"You're preaching to the converted, boy," Rings responded, not unkindly.

"Prancing paladins," Belgin said bitterly. He was a rakishly classy man, his clothes a cut above the rest of the party's. "Paladins're stiff where a body's supposed to be loose, and loose where a body's supposed to be stiff. Unnatural creatures." He punctuated his soliloquy with a deft movement of one hand, weaving his napkin through the tines of his fork.

"Exactly!" Noph enthused. "Hypocrites!"

"Not us," Belgin said, a sardonic smile on his face. With a snap of his fingers, the Sharker made the napkin slide from the fork and disappear into a silken sleeve. "We tell you ahead of time we're cheats and liars and scoundrels."

"So, how did you reach Eldrinpar?" Noph asked. "Surely you've got some swashbuckling tales."

Ingrar said, "Tales seem less thrilling when you've lived through them." He gestured at his blind eyes.

"Well, I had some adventures on the way," Noph said. "We fought our way through Undermountain—the realm of Halaster the Mad Mage—and then had to defeat an army of fiends to get to a portal, and then came face to face with the mage-king of Doegan, a creature that—"

"You want a story?" interrupted Shar. The sorrow was gone from her, and she leaned enticingly against Noph. He was surprised how warm and, well, flexible her leather tunic felt. "You want to know how we got here? You want a story to end all stories?"

"Well, at least a story to end my story," Noph said, blushing.

The others laughed, except for Entreri, who scowled at the young man. Shar noticed. She moved a thin arm snakelike along Noph's chest.

"All right, but be warned: We're cheats and scoundrels and liars," she purred. "Believe the particulars to your peril."

The word "peril" had never sounded so good. "I'm— I'm game."

"Yes, you are." Shar laughed lightly and cast a glance across Noph at the assassin. She idly stroked the blond fuzz that lined the young man's chin. "It all began with a fellow named Orim Redbeard, captain of the *Black Dragon*. He had taken a disliking to us Sharkers—"

"Sharkers?" Noph squeaked as he felt a certain presence beneath the table. He cleared his throat. "Wh-Who are the Sharkers?"

"Us. Crew members of the *Kissing Shark*, fabled ship of Blackfingers Ralingor. Redbeard had lots of reasons to hate us. First among them, though, was that we knew his beard was really white and only dyed with a mix of rust and milk."

"Your leaving him at the altar might have been another reason," added Rings dryly.

"Shut up. I'm telling this story," Shar advised. "Now, whatever his reasons, Redbeard was after Blackfingers and the *Kissing Shark*. He couldn't catch us, though. We can be . . . quite slippery when wet."

Noph gulped at that. "G-Go on."

Shar twined a finger through Noph's hair, but she was gazing directly at Entreri. "Some men are threatened by things they can't hold onto. Some try anything to keep their distance. Redbeard hired a sorcerer—a tiny twig of a man. What was his name? Winebreath Anglebutt?"

"Windborn Axlegrease?"

"Wimprod Antibody?"

"Something like that. Anyway, this Warthog Antfarm ran us aground near Tenteeth Point. The hull—six-inches of oak and hard as steel—was staved on the first spit of land and hooked by the second. Then the storm set to chewing us to pieces. And if that weren't enough, in comes Redbeard and his *Black Dragon*, and his mage holds them offshore—Redbeard wasn't seaman enough to do it in that storm—and they launched flaming ballistae at us."

"Fire arrows," broke in Entreri. "They were only fire arrows, of the very sort they used against the *Morning Bird*."

"A man such as you shouldn't quibble about size, Artemis," Shar replied elegantly, sneering past Noph. "These were ballistae if they weren't comets sent from Tempus himself. You don't know. You weren't there."

"I was," Entreri replied, as softly as before. "I watched as the seven of you survivors climbed to shore."

"You what?"

"Didn't you fight back?" interrupted Noph.

Shar managed to look both offended and stumped. "Fight back?" She glanced quickly to her comrades. "Sure, we fought back, didn't we? Belgin, tell the boy how we fought back."

"Well," he said, considering, "Shar, here, has a secret weapon . . . an exceptional secret weapon—"

"She's inflatable," Rings supplied in a rush.

Shar glared at the dwarf.

"Inflatable?" Noph wondered aloud, staring.

Shar's irritation turned on him.

"Yes, indeed," Rings gabbled. "Saved us all from drowning. We just held onto Shar and floated from the burning *Shark*."

"My word," said Noph, still staring.

"And that's not the half of it," Belgin continued. "She became large enough to catch wind, and carried us on a collision course with the *Black Dragon*."

Noph looked up at last. "What about the ballistae? Didn't they keep shooting ballistae at you?"

"Too frightened, my boy," Belgin said smoothly. "By this time Shar was enormous, you understand. Any pirate who saw her attacking his ship would think he was being boarded by Umberlee the Bitch Queen, herself."

"And Redbeard being a virgin and all—" Rings added.

"A virgin?"

"The man had no more keel than a dinghy," Ingrar added with such calm aplomb he seemed almost mournful.

"I, on the other hand, supplied the raft of us with a right impressive keel," Belgin boasted.

"A daggerboard, if you ask me," Rings replied.

"And you would know, sinking like an anchor," Belgin sneered. "Dwarves, you'll find, son, float like stones— and are just as dense."

"What did you do when you reached the *Black Dragon?*" Noph asked, looking with new admiration at Shar.

Her initial consternation was giving way to amusement. Flicking a smile toward Artemis, who irritably endured it all, Shar leaned her legendary weapons against Noph and said, "I crushed them!"

Noph recoiled slightly, his eyes wide. "A virgin pirate, crushed in the bosoms of Umberlee!" he croaked out in amazement. "That sure is some swash and buckle!"

This final naive comment was too much for any of them, and the pirates exploded with laughter, lifting their flagons in a salute.

Noph scratched his head. "You killed Captain Redbeard and his whole crew and sank his ship when Shar inflated herself?"

The Sharkers nodded, struggling to stifle their mirth.

"Of course not," said Entreri irritably. "The only ship destroyed that night was the *Kissing Shark*, the only thing inflated was this ridiculous story, and the only crew slain were the Sharkers, with seven liars swimming ashore."

Noph blushed at the reprimand. "Seven? That's you four, plus Anvil, and two others. Who were the other two?"

The pirates' countenances lost their mirth. There was silence for a moment. Then Belgin said, "Well, there was Brindra, a good comrade of all of us, whom we lost battling a fiend beyond the city walls. And there was Kurthe. He was killed by this man, here, in fair combat." He stared hard at the impassive face of Entreri for a moment, then turned back to Noph. "Kurthe was a Konigheimer, big and tough, and had it in his head he was our leader. Master Entreri disagreed."

"What about your captain—Captain Blackfingers?" asked Noph. "Did he die, too?"

"No—well, yes. It's hard to say," Belgin hedged, hiding his expression behind the lifted flagon. "I'd not be surprised if the captain made a return, here, sometime soon."

"You might as well tell him," said Ingrar. "Master Entreri has taken Kurthe's place, and maybe this lad can take the place of Anvil or Brindra. If not, the captain is as good as dead, anyway."

"What are you talking about?" asked Entreri coldly.

Belgin blinked. He glanced soberly at his comrades and gestured to them. "We, such as we are, *are* Captain Blackfingers Ralingor."

"What?" asked Noph. "All of you, together?"

"We seven," Ingrar said, and the others nodded. "A kind of joint-stock company."

Noph was now thoroughly confused. "You mean there never was any Captain Blackfingers? You made him up?"

Rings glanced at Shar. "No, there was such a man. But he died, and we didn't want to spread it around. So Belgin here came up with the idea of pretending he was still alive."

Entreri's features darkened. "Interesting that you kept this from me all this while."

It was Shar who responded, her voice silky and reproving. "Just as you kept your identity secret from us."

"So, that is why Redbeard was so keen on slaying you. He knew who you were," Entreri said.

"Aye," the dwarf replied sullenly. "The good captain did many offenses to earn Redbeard's wrath."

Belgin nudged the dwarf. "Including giving him the scare that turned his famous beard white—"

Rings reddened, holding back laughter. "It seems the man wasn't prepared for a dwarf to crawl up his privy, while he was . . . enthroned. I still miss that spiked helmet."

The group laughed heavily, except for Entreri, who

kept his eyes on Sharessa, his lips drawn in a tight line. The dwarf, tears wringing from the creases of his eyes, called for another round.

"Well, I'll happily take the place of Brindra or Anvil, or both," Noph said. "I'm one of you, now. I'm part of Captain Blackfingers!"

"Not so fast, lad. You've got to prove yourself. There's a kind of initiation to pass before you can become a part of this legend," Shar said.

"Did Master Entreri pass the initiation?"

"Sure," Shar said, peering at her employer. Her voice dripped contempt. "The main test and more. He's a true pirate, a swashbuckling rogue—that's him."

"Well, then," Noph said, drawing himself up with a breath, "I'm ready, whatever the test might be."

Shar stroked his chin. "Let's see, the first measure of a pirate's got to be his sea legs. The only way to test that's to clamber the lines during the height of a midnight storm. Not just the ratlines, now, but the shrouds and stays. I mean shinny out to the tip of the forespar, climb the ropes to all the spars of the foremast, and all of the mizzen, and main, and the stern mast, and back down the sheet to the tiller. Mind you, the tops've got to be rolling and pitching within inches of a fifty-foot sea on both sides the whole time."

"And then," said Rings, "you've got to go below to the bilges and sleep half-sunk in that icy, sloshing mess."

"And if you're not asleep before the storm's done, you've got to wait for the next midnight squall and do it all over."

Noph looked green. "Master Entreri did this?"

"Oh, yes, all the while the *Black Dragon* was tailing us, he did. And more," Ingrar replied, somewhat truthfully.

Noph glanced admiringly at Entreri, who ignored him. "That's just to test your sea legs," continued Shar. "But a pirate's not just a seaman. A pirate's got to be as loyal to his mates as he is vicious to his foes. To be a pirate, you've got to kill a dozen of the crew's enemies, all with your bare hands."

"And immersed in freezing water," piped up Belgin.

"With sharks and barracudas in it," added Rings.

Noph swallowed audibly. His voice was weak. "And Master Entreri did all this?"

"Oh, yes. Once we landed here in Doegan, he began slaying fiends, on land, in air, in freezing water. If it hadn't been for him, we'd all be dead ten times over."

Noph nodded. "That's a tall order."

"It gets taller," said Shar. "A pirate's not just a seaman who knows his friends from his enemies. A pirate's also an incomplete creature—missing part of himself."

"You mean, like a wooden leg or a hook or something?"

"Well, yes. Or something even dearer. All of us has had a chunk ripped away."

"It's usually the softest part that gets torn out," Belgin said, "your heart or your head or your stomach or your guts or your spleen—"

"What part was it for you, Belgin?" asked Noph.

The gambler hissed a sigh. "I don't know what organ you'd call it, but it's the part that used to feel surprise, awe, wonder—the part that responds when you confront something bigger than you could've imagined. I'm not surprised by anything, now. You could rip off your skin and emerge a crocodile, and in the middle of biting off my head, I'd think, 'Hmm, the boy turned out to be a crocodile.' "

"What about the rest of you?" Noph asked.

"My eyes," Ingrar remarked with a strange calm. "Though I feel I've gained something in the bargain. I can't see the surface of things anymore, but I sense what lies beneath. For instance, Belgin, you're thinking you'll go sharping tonight, and you've got a marked deck of cards in your pocket, the crowns up your sleeves; Noph, you're aching for our dear Shadow. You're not thinking she's a cobra, but she is, so you might want to take your hand off her thigh."

Noph complied, blushing, and shifted away from Shar. He noticed Belgin looked just as uncomfortable.

"How'd you know?" the sharper asked. "Some kind of psionic—"

"I used my other senses. Your marked deck still smells like mackerel from the night you won the fishing boat. And your sleeves have been dragging."

Belgin crossed flowing silks over his chest. "How would a clever fellow like you feel about joining me at the table tonight?"

"Certainly," Ingrar replied. "As for the rest of you, it's smells, mostly. You know how they say an animal can smell fear? Well, I can smell just about every emotion coming from you."

"What about me?" asked Rings. "What am I thinking?"

"You're thinking you'll have another ale."

In the midst of the ensuing laughter, Rings waved a stout hand to the waiter, calling for a final round. Entreri stared hard at Ingrar. "And I?" he said softly. "Do you know what I'm thinking?"

Ingrar turned his blind eyes toward the assassin, his face troubled. "I . . . I think so. No, no, I don't," he amended hastily.

Sharessa's face soured. "Well, what's been ripped out of me would have to have been my heart. It got shredded early on. I'd not have survived with it."

Noph and Entreri both cast sidelong glances at the beautiful woman.

Rings spoke up. "Back there in the forest, I lost my conscience. Always before, there was a split second pause before I killed. Among the fiends, I learned to kill by reflex."

"What about you, Master Entreri?" asked Noph.

The assassin did not look at any of them. He merely

stared ahead, into the empty spaces between swaying fronds. "Long before I met any of you, perhaps before some of you were born, I murdered my own soul." He smiled painfully. "It's been a much smoother journey since." After a deep breath, the assassin asked, "And, what about you, Kastonoph Nesher? What will you lose?"

"I'll cut off my ear this very night to become part of Captain Blackfingers Ralingor!" Noph enthused, but his comrades only sighed and shook their heads.

The waiter arrived with the last round of drinks and set them, careful not to spill, before the patrons.

"Now that the confessions and confabulations are finished," Entreri said, "I have some business to discuss—among those whom I've hired. Noph, if you don't mind?"

The young man looked injured. "But I'm one of you."

"Are you pledged to slay Lady Eidola, like the rest of us?"

Noph hung his head. His bangs drooped over his eyes. Without touching his drink, he stood and strode out to the street.

"We've told you of our secret past," Shar said, her eyes narrowing suspiciously. "What about yours, Master Entreri?"

The little man gazed levelly at her. "What is there to tell? I am an assassin. I enjoy my work, and excel at it. Many of the famous persons who have disappeared or turned up dead in the past years have been my work."

"We guessed that much from what the paladin said at the fountain," Shar retorted. "But we still don't know anything about you."

"If you know that much, you know everything you need to know about me," said Entreri, his voice hushed but no less emphatic. "More information will take some . . . effort on your part." He stared significantly at the woman. "Now, there has been a slight change of plan. To find Lady Eidola, we need to find the bloodforge of Doegan."

"What are you talking about?" sputtered Rings, a native of this land.

"I am talking about conspiracy, my stout fellow. My employer told me that Eidola was kidnapped by a bloodforge-conjured army and that she is held here in Doegan. Someone with access to Doegan's bloodforge must hold her. Find the bloodforge, and we find the lady.

"You've no idea what you say," Rings hissed. "The bloodforge is the heart of Doegan's military might. It is the best guarded weapon in the arsenal!"

"And I am the greatest assassin in Faerûn, and you are my handpicked strike force."

"I'm in," said Ingrar immediately. "And before you decide a blind man can't do you any good on this mission, let me advise you not to drink this last round. It has been poisoned." As the others drew hands away from their flagons, the blind pirate said, "It's not actually a poison, but a sleep agent. I imagine the owner of this place plans to turn us over to the mage-king's forces."

The assassin gave the blind man a frank stare, then nodded. "Thanks for the warning." With a flick of his wrist, Entreri flung outward a batch of tiny white pills, one of which fell, bubbling, into each drink. Then he hoisted his own flagon and drank it to the dregs. "Don't worry: one of those pills could purify a whole lake."

The others were wary. Ingrar sniffed his drink, seemed mildly impressed, and drained it. After that, the others followed suit, each setting down his or her empty flagon with the words, "I'm in."

Rings downed his own drink, pledged his loyalty, and then, for good measure, downed Noph's, too.

## Interlude

# *Concupiscence*

I'm mesmerized by you.

I can't help it. I know I should be solemn as we carry the old dead mercenary out to the dock, but you're right in front of me. You're right against me. You're holding his thigh, and I'm holding his knee, and you're leaning hard against me.

"*. . . my heart. It got shredded early on. . . .*"

What a bitter fate, if you stopped loving just before I started.

Now I know why he was called Anvil: he's as heavy as one. Still, if he'd been light, you'd not be pressed up against me now, as we stagger past the crates and up the splintery dock.

There's the dinghy, ahead. The small waves of the harbor slap against its gunwales. It's a narrow, long boat, what they build down here, and I'm thinking we'll need a shoehorn to get Anvil into it. I'm also thinking you must need a shoehorn to slip into those pants.

You were crawling all over me through lunch. Ingrar's told me you're using me to get at Entreri, but I think you really do like me. And what's not to like? Maybe once I've climbed the rigging and killed a dozen foes, I'll be able to tear my heart out and give it to you and teach you to love again.

Listen to me. A day ago I would have pledged my loyalty to Aleena Paladinstar. Now it's you, Sharessa Stagwood. You're opposites, but the same—mysterious, unattainable, untame.

It's a strain to hold Anvil this way, low and over the edge of the dock. Loose on three. Damn! I did it on two. I'm losing hold, anyway. The others drop him, and you almost follow him, over into the drink. I grab you and pull you back. For a second, you're clinging tight to me, and I'm glad.

"Get away from her, boy!" It is Entreri, the assassin. He yanks you back. You seem startled, dismayed. He's jealous and . . . angry that he's jealous.

Then you break away from him, too. You can't be held. You stand apart from us, hands on your hips, and watch as the others pile oil-soaked wood around Anvil's head and feet and stuff it between his body and his arms. On top of it all, they lay out a rag of tarp, and Anvil's sword. Then, with a grunt, Rings shoves the dinghy out from the dock.

The boat glides, dark and silent, away from us, out of the wind shadow of the dock and into the higher waves of the seaward breeze. It's quickly beyond my throwing arm, and then twice that far. The assassin stoops down, lights a torch, and wings the thing out over the bay. The fiery brand plummets like a shooting star and fire flares up.

"Farewell to a part of Captain Blackfingers Ralingor," Ring says solemnly.

As I stand there among you and the others, the rest of the captain, I think how fine it will be to be a pirate, too.

Who knows? You might even trust me with your shoehorn.

## Chapter 5
# Conchology

Lord Ikavi Garkim looked up from the interrogation. The man seated before him had been trembling and sobbing, spewing out an endless string of half-truths and untruths, never approaching the fact his mind shouted: the pirates had eaten like kings at this very pub just yesterday.

"If spies had been here, I would have poisoned them—"

"All right. Shut up," Garkim interrupted with a chopping movement of his hand.

There was something else beckoning to him, an odor

on the wind. It smelled like a beached leviathan, the stench of something once hidden in black brine but now exposed to sun and air. It was an odor of death.

The mage-king. Always, Aetheric remained in contact with his right-hand man, as though Garkim were but another stone golem. Sometimes he could feel the mage-king gazing out through his own eyes, speaking through his own mouth. But almost never did Aetheric send his summons this way, a pungent and piteous scent. It was as though the mage-king himself were poisoned and dying.

Garkim released the barkeep's shoulder, only then realizing he had grabbed hold of it. He stepped toward the door, though the motion was more a stagger. Whatever black humors coursed, paralyzing, through the mage-king coursed through Garkim, as well.

He has made me, Garkim realized. His death would unmake me, just as surely.

The clatter of an overturned plant stand broke into Garkim's reverie. He stumbled out the door, calling to the proprietor: "I go now. The mage-king is finished with you." He turned and shambled away.

Behind him, the man's piteous laments only increased, as though Garkim had just pronounced a death sentence. If the mage-king truly were poisoned, it would be a death sentence for all Doegan....

The palace. It was there, just there, above the rankling horizon of adobe and timbers. It was visible from every alley and court of the city. If only his legs would carry him that far.

Garkim knew this city—every shop window and alleyway and secret door—but it suddenly seemed alien to him. It was not a city anymore—not *his* city—but an endless maze of mud and dun. Garkim moved along the street as if in a dream. The midday sun was gray despite the clear sky.

The city usually knew him, too. Today, though, it

recoiled from him. It knew something was terribly wrong. Mar and Ffolk alike disappeared in the lane before him, draining into whatever niches presented themselves. Hovels leaned away from the staggering lord. Bleached awnings hung dead still in the dread air. Even the mud street sucked in its belly as though shying beneath a creeping scorpion.

What could it be? Was the mage-king dying? Had his body endured the final assault from the bloodforge? Had the paladins returned with some cursed hammer of Tyr that could smash through the wall of the mage-king's abode?

If the mage-king fell, all Doegan would fall.

He could hear nothing. Lips moved in the shadows of drawn curtains, wagon wheels tumbled hastily out of sight, but he could hear not a whisper. There was only a strange, omnipresent groan, as of the world itself rolling over in restless sleep.

The city fell away in ten thousand numb steps and at last, suddenly, Garkim staggered into the blue shadow of the palace.

He crossed the stair bridge above the dry moat and bulled his way past the gate guards who had stepped in to bar his way. There was a touch of Aetheric's own strength in this melancholy that had settled over Lord Garkim; one of the guards went down clutching cracked ribs, and the other was knocked unconscious by an errant elbow.

Seeing what had happened to the first guards, the second pair let Garkim through without requesting a password. He took no notice of them. They were like roaches clinging to the curved belly of the tunnel he walked. The very stones were warped by the Mage-King's deep, horrific sorrow.

How could the guards not sense it? How could they be so oblivious to this recursive dread?

The curvature seemed greater with each step, until

individual stones stretched in eerie shapes around Garkim. It was as though he were walking within a glass globe. The world outside was bent into utter absurdity. His eyes could not tell him whether he stood in the crescent hallway before the audience chamber or on the highest parapet atop the tower. But he didn't need eyes. The same putrid imperative that gagged his gills told him which direction to walk.

Curved glimpses of windows and sunlit stones receded behind him like water down a drain. A vast cold blackness loomed up. The audience chamber. In silence, he was swallowed.

*Come farther, Garkim. Come farther.*

He did. In the void, he glimpsed a tiny form, wriggling with thousands of dim fingers. A sea anemone. The creature's tendrils stretched outward into worms, into thin tentacles, into encircling bands of wet muscle. Still Garkim continued. The coiling, ropy lines thickened, slowly squeezing out the darkness, the air. In two more steps, the ever-grasping creature encompassed the whole of creation.

One last step, and Garkim stopped. In that final movement, the infinite intertwined tentacles resolved into smooth, clean flesh. Human flesh. A man. Aetheric III. He floated in darkness before Garkim, a huge muscled man with dense golden curls atop his head, piercing blue eyes, a nose slightly curled like the beak of a sea hawk, and sad-edged lips. His naked skin was as golden as his hair. This was how he wanted Garkim to see him.

Beautiful. Tragic. Glorious. Powerful.

*It is time for you to know our mind, Ikavi Garkim.*

Unsure what else to do, face to face with the mortal image of his master, Garkim knelt and bowed his head. "As you wish, Mage-King Aetheric. Speak, and I will know."

The rich voice filled his mind, consumed him with its words.

*We brought Lady Eidola here. It was no other. Not Waterdhavian nobles. Not the Fallen Temple. Not the Unseen. It was we. We used our bloodforge to conjure warriors and gate them into the chapel of Piergeiron's Palace.*

A chill ran down Garkim's spine. It dismayed him that he had not even guessed this.

*There is much more you do not know about us, little one. Some of it we tell you now.*

In an effort to silence his thoughts, Garkim asked, "Why? Why did you kidnap Lady Eidola?"

*We kidnapped her for this very hour. The hour of our deliverance—or our demise. Have you not seen how our people are ill, languishing beneath this oppressive contagion?*

"I have more than seen, Your Highness," Garkim replied, peeling down the edges of his collar. "I, too, am infected, though I have not yet grown weak, like the others."

*The disease is brought on by the bloodforge. You knew that. The disease first attacked only us. We have, these many decades, absorbed all the twisting evil of the bloodforge into our own body, so saving our people.*

"Praise be to thee, Your Highness."

*But it is too much now. The bloodforge has grown ravenous. It has eaten holes through us, and its terrible teeth gnash outward upon our people. Its poisons creep into their blood, slowing them, filling them with fever, transforming their flesh. We know what it does to them, to you, for already it did these things to us.*

"We have spoken of this already, my king," Garkim said. "I know what has brought the Gray Malaise, and what has, for that matter, brought the very armies of hell to batter our gates. I know that only with the bloodforge can we fight the tanar'ri, though its very use makes us weaker." He had grown as pale as a sea slug. "So, then, why use the bloodforge to steal away Eidola

of Neverwinter? Did not that only worsen the artifact's
cravings, and bring more fiends?"

*It was meant to bring us new armies to fight our old
foes. It brought us paladins and pirates.*

*As long as Eidola of Neverwinter remained in my
dungeons, beneath this very tank, more warriors would
have arrived in these lands, armies of them. They would
have fought the fiend war for us. In time, the fiends
would have been slaughtered. Then we would have relaxed our defenses, and the bloodforge would once more
have grown quiet. Such was my plan.*

"What has gone wrong?"

*The Paladinson has fallen into a deep coma. Were he
awake, he would have mustered the greatest fleet in
Faerûn to come here in search of his lost bride. They
would have come and fought fiends for us and driven
them all back to the Abyss. Instead, the loveless mage
Khelben Blackstaff has sent only one small group, whose
number was nearly halved before they even arrived—
two dead, and Paladinstar remaining to tend her father.
Now even the foolish youth Kastonoph has left them. We
cannot throw back the fiends with such pitiful numbers
as these. The Blackstaff does not prize his master's bride
as he ought.*

"But surely when these paladins fail, the Blackstaff
will send this fleet you speak of—"

*We have not time to wait for these Tyr-kissers to fail.
The fiends have found another route into the city, through
a deep and ancient labyrinth of dwarf tunnels. To close
all of them off would require a use of the bloodforge that
would be instantly lethal for every creature in Doegan.
The fiends will find their way into the city, and soon.*

*You will muster all of our forces and array them to protect the palace. Already our energies are so strained that
we cannot keep track of these paladins and pirates. They
are the least of our worries, inconsequential now. They are
nothing beside these armies of fiends.*

"The fiends will not reach you, Highness."

*You guard not us, but the bloodforge. If it is lost, all is lost. We ourselves will fight to our death to defend it.*

"When will the fiends arrive, Highness?"

*Before dusk, tomorrow.*

"Then this truly is the hour of our deliverance, or our demise."

There was something unutterably mournful in the mind of the mage-king, the sort of sweet, quiet, bitter reflection of a monarch dying even as his warriors won the war. *It is the apocalypse. If the bloodforge is stolen, it will be gained at the price of our own life, of your life, Ikavi, and that of every citizen in Doegan.*

*Let there be no more Ffolk, no more Mar. We, Aetheric III, are Ffolk, and yet we could not have ruled without your aid, Ikavi Garkim—and you are Mar. Let there be no more Ffolk, no more Mar, but only warriors of Doegan. We shall triumph together, or die together.*

*But warriors are not enough. For the fiends to be beaten back and defeated, we will have to become far more than ever we have been. We must be transformed. We must emerge from this poisoned chrysalis into new, winged life. We must transcend.*

*Either way, Aetheric III, mage-king of Doegan, will forever cease to be.*

*Interlude*

# Congratulations

So much for being mesmerized.

All right, all right, so you got the girl already. You two could be a little quieter in the next room, so the rest of us could get some sleep. Of course, Rings and Belgin are making as much noise with their snoring, and Ingrar's probably asleep, too.

Congratulations, Entreri. I doubt she'll be getting a new heart from you.

And what the hell is it with these dried sponges for pillows? I feel like I'm sleeping on the bottom of the damned sea.

## Chapter 6

# Contention

Next afternoon, Miltiades was more grim-faced than usual as he strode slowly ahead of his men. The adobe slums around him looked as run-down as he felt. Still no luck.

After the fiasco at the Mar funeral, Miltiades and the paladins had headed back toward the palace to get washed and rested. En route, though, Lord Garkim and his guards had caught up to them. Too battle weary to offer resistance, the paladins were quickly surrounded and slowly questioned about every detail of their encounter with the pirates earlier. Once that whole battle had been reviewed, Garkim had grilled the warriors about their antics at the Mar funeral. It was clear that Garkim, a Mar himself, was angered by the attack, but had orders to take no action yet.

At last, chastened, burned, and defeated, the paladins returned to the palace, where their wounds were treated and their aching bodies bathed. Next morning, healed and polished, the warriors returned to their grueling search for the Fallen Temple and Eidola. By that afternoon, they had walked every major thoroughfare and most of the minor ones. Trandon all the while wore the pendant Khelben Arunsun had given them. It was supposed to glow anywhere within a mile of Lady Eidola, but the rock had remained dark.

Kern seemed more disappointed than the rest. "I probably ruined the magic of that thing when I wore it. Sometimes being antimagical is a real nuisance."

"And sometimes it's a great boon," Trandon replied. He pinched the chain in two fingers and gently lifted the amulet from his chest, letting it dangle in the air before him. "Besides, I think it's still magical." His eyes followed the last light of day as it shimmered across the gold filigree. "It doesn't look disrupted."

"You don't know any more about magic than I do," snapped Kern. He stopped in his tracks, dust whuffing up from his feet. "I'm sorry. Frustration has always been my greatest foe, the one emotion that can master me. Forgive my outburst."

Trandon waved the apology away. "There's nothing to forgive. We all are anxious about Eidola."

Kern lifted his gaze toward the blue sky, giving itself over without sunset to a silken black. "She's probably not even here. It wouldn't surprise me if our host lied to us about her presence in the city."

"That wouldn't surprise me either," Trandon replied. He let the stone sink slowly back to his chest. "But, for some reason, I feel she *is* here, only warded by some particularly powerful enchantment. If only we could—"

He broke off midsentence, seeing that Miltiades had halted before them and signaled them to silence. With soundless tread, Kern, Trandon, and Jacob edged toward the silver paladin, who stood with his head cocked, listening.

"What is it?" Jacob whispered.

Miltiades silenced him with an emphatic wave of his hand.

They listened. At first, they heard only the hushed whispers of a Mar slum. From beyond that came the distant bustle of the city. Beneath those everyday sounds, though, was a strange wet rumble. The noise was quiet but seemed to come from everywhere—the streets, the walls, the shops, the sewers. . . .

"Something's coming up!" Miltiades rasped, uncertain.

Next moment, two warhammers, a sword, and a staff were hefted, ready for whatever horror might arise.

And arise it did, in a thousand thousand places—from the trash pit at the end of the street, and the weed-choked culvert at the crossroads, and the shattered sewer grate. . . . The rumbling grew deafening, as though whatever approached was using the very face of Toril as a war drum. Then, through every crack in the mud roadway and every well or pit or grave came a reek somewhere between offal and brimstone—a hot smell as if the sewers themselves were boiling.

Columns of steam formed. Shards of mud burst outward. Things emerged. Iron floodgates that had endured decades of monsoons shattered and spun away, ringing like claxons. Into the space where they had been, horrors scrambled: serrated horns, spiked sagittal crests, eyes as long and thin as scythe blades, jaws that were no more than bone and daggers, bodies of wire and scale, clawed talons, stinging tails. . . . And these were only the nearby beasts—blood-hued monstrosities that clambered up from the culvert beside Miltiades. In the distance, he glimpsed grasping tentacles, hairless rat tails, vast wings of skin. . . .

"Tyr aid us! Fiends!" Miltiades shouted in the midst of a mighty swing of his warhammer.

The gleaming head of the weapon struck a demon's horned nose, driving the spike back through the thing's skull and into its brain. It fell, lavender gore jetting from ears and eyes.

"Stay tight! Backs together!" Miltiades shouted needlessly. The charge of fiends had already formed the others into a defensive circle. Miltiades had no more time for orders; the next fiend had arrived.

It was meaty and pink and muscular, and it brandished a cat-o'-nine-tails in a three-fingered fist. The bits of iron and shattered glass tied into the leather thongs glowed with fiendish fire, swarming up behind the beast's fat-lipped grin. Then lashes descended and wrapped themselves around Miltiades. Iron and glass sank in, stinging wasps. They pinged against his silver armor and burned through leather straps and muslin pads.

Miltiades roared, struggling to yank his arms free from his sides. The beast roared, too, or laughed. It hauled on the cat-o'-nine-tails with one arm, spinning the paladin, and brought down its saber.

The sword keened through the air and struck the head of the blessed hammer, which swung free as Miltiades whirled. The hammer batted back the blade but missed the pink meat of the monster's face. In that moment, Miltiades could think only one thing: Where hammers fail, let calmer heads prevail.

*Crack.* He had never head-butted a fiend before.

There was an inarticulate curse as the wall of muscle buckled and fell, senseless, to the ground.

"Maybe I do have a hard head, after all," he gasped before meeting the next onslaught.

Beside him, Kern was having no easier time of it. He still battled his first fiend, a spell-warded scorpion-man whose poison-dripping tail jagged like lightning. The red-scaled creature fought with a berserker's fury, a wizard's magic, a warrior's twin scimitars, and a scorpion's mesmerizing tail. It was all Kern could do to grab a breath between swings of his gleaming hammer.

The maul cracked off the darting tail, knocking it aside but failing to crush it. Green sparks around the hammerhead showed why. Magical protections. Kern had no time to watch where the tail went: the creature swung one of its scimitars. Kern blocked, flinging up the butt of the hammer. He pulled the attack with his back swing.

The other scimitar descended. It bit through the gold mail glittering on Kern's shoulder and found flesh beneath.

Kern ducked toward the blade and flung it off with a bloodstained brassard. He kicked out hard. His boot rang off a pectoral scale.

A pair of the thing's eight legs reached out to snatch him off his feet and drag him down.

Kern leapt back from the snatching claws, turned a flip, and kicked the scorpion man in the jaw. It shuddered, stunned for a moment. Kern landed in a crouch. He came up swinging. His hammer cracked the same spot his foot had just hit. The beast shuddered again and shook its head to clear it. Kern helped. The blow that finally smashed through the magical defenses also smashed the bug-man's cranium, and sent the thing collapsing like a struck tent.

"Tanar'ri," Kern spat, along with some of his own blood.

These were the worst opponents in all the worlds, creatures so lawless their every move was unpredictable. They routinely killed more of their own in battle than of their foe—and still won.

A spidery thing ambled in toward Kern. He bounced his hammer haft in one hand and counted the number of enemies they now had: the Fallen Temple, the mage-king, Artemis Entreri and his pirates, the hosts of the Abyss, and the coming darkness. If they stayed any longer, they'd be fighting the whole world.

The spider-thing—an eight-foot-tall beast with the blood-grizzled body of a greater wolf—lunged.

Kern hurled the hammer head at the beast's gaping jowls. Once again, green magic sparked around the weapon, deflecting it.

The jaws clamped onto Kern's bloody shoulder. Huge black legs strained backward, lifting him from the ground. Wolf teeth pressed through his golden armor and bruised his flesh. Four of the spider's legs wrapped his torso and clutched him against the prickly abdomen. The paladin's warhammer was uselessly fouled in the tightening legs.

*This is the end*, Kern realized with strange calm, clutched to the belly of the monster. *This beast will squeeze me to death. I should not be surprised—an antimagical man battling a purely magical being. . . .*

The beast went still around him. It dropped, smashing Kern beneath its body. The wolf torso shattered on his chest and fell in petrified, coal-black chunks.

Kern scrambled to his feet. All around him he saw fragments of the brittle, frozen body of the wolf-spider.

*An antimagical man battling a purely magical being . . .*

That was how he must fight these monsters—get in close enough that his very presence froze their sorcerous hearts.

Letting out an unseemly whoop, the paladin swung his hammer high, beckoning the next comers.

Jacob heard the shout. He stood to one side of Kern, but was presently occupied with his own troubles—namely a scaly-skinned lizard-man with a double-ended trident. The slit-pupilled fiend had already won past Jacob's sword dozens of times, and the man's belly was spotted with cuts and jabs. Sweat poured from his face to his neck and ran cruel fingers into his wounds.

The three barbed points of the lizard-man's trident flashed past Jacob's slow sword and spitted him across the middle. Jacob gasped. Blood rimmed his lips as the thing yanked him forward. Its forked tongue flickered in anticipation.

This is nonsense, Jacob thought, writhing on the skewer. I needn't die like this.

The lizard-man hoisted Jacob on the trident and held him up to an appraising eye. Its tongue tickled along the man's bloody cheek. The monster opened its jaws, set with tidy rows of conical teeth.

Jacob placed a hand almost tenderly on the creature's neck. Before its teeth could bite down, its head rolled loosely forward and dropped to the ground, revealing a cleanly sheered neck. The stump was cut at an angle, like the pruned branch of a hedge.

Jacob yanked the impaling tines from his gut and stepped away as the body followed its head to the ground.

Trandon, meanwhile, was busy fighting an everreaching land squid. His quarterstaff was fine for pummeling hard heads and tripping up ankles and jabbing bellies, but the writhing squid had none of these. Each blow from Trandon's staff landed with an unimpressive thud. The spineless creature oozed away, cushioning the attack to a soft halt.

This is like battling a mud hole, Trandon thought. Except, of course, that mud holes don't lash back.

Trandon reeled away from the slap of a tentacle. Suckers popped as they peeled from his neck. They left a line of circular red welts.

"Oh, bother," Trandon said, slapping a hand to his neck.

He glanced to both sides, then pointed a finger and growled something. Black lightning crackled out from his staff, sizzled into and around one of the monster's probing tentacles, and made a smoky *boom* within the beast. The land squid deflated into a smoldering puddle.

Still, the monsters were many, and darkness had fallen.

## Chapter 7
## *Conflict*

Night was stealing into the palace as Noph crowded with Shar and the others behind the drapes of the great hall. They had arrived here by way of the kitchen garbage chute, and so had slithered through mounds of fish tails, shucked clamshells, greasy cuttlebones, and jellyfish heads.

They stank like the mage-king, himself.

Noph felt especially bad for Ingrar, who had the keenest nose among them. Of late, he could tell what was in a locked room merely by sniffing beneath the door. Just now, Ingrar couldn't smell anything but the remains of the mage-king's lunch.

"The emperor will keep the bloodforge well guarded and near him," Entreri said. "If Noph's memory of the palace serves, beyond the great hall is a wide, crescent-shaped corridor that connects all the ceremonial spaces. The high double doors at the center of the crescent give into the audience chamber. Beyond it lies the mage-king's personal quarters—his tank. The bloodforge must be there."

"But I told you," Noph said, "there's no way to get at the mage-king through the audience chamber. The tank takes up one whole wall. The glass is impervious to all attacks, magical or mundane. The water is poisonous. And even if the glass could be broken and the water were safe, you'd still be swept away and drowned."

"Impervious is an overrated word. The bloodforge is in there with him; I'm sure of it. If we have to drain the tank and beach the big fish, then we have to. Besides, I have ways of breaching the unbreachable wall and surviving the flood and the poison. I have this." Entreri twirled a flat silver plate in his fingertips.

"What is it?" Shar asked, leaning close against him.

"A little thieving device—the fellow selling them came from a place call Sigil. Stick this on a wall or window, and it creates a gate to the other side. The thief can stick a hand through and snatch whatever he can reach. Of course an assassin such as myself might be more likely to throw a dagger through—"

"You're going to throw a dagger at a fifty-foot-tall squid-man?" Noph interrupted.

"Something a little more subtle," Entreri assured him.

"First we have to reach the chamber—have to get past an army of guards between here and there," Belgin groused. The sharper's face was looking more drawn and sickly than usual. "There's probably two outside the great hall, four outside the audience chamber, eight outside the mage-king's tank, and between sixteen and thirty-two guarding the bloodforge."

"Perhaps now, but not in a few moments from now," Entreri said. "I've planned a diversion." He nodded toward the doors of the great hall. As if on cue, shouts rose outside.

"Fire! Fire in the treasury!"

The pirates and Noph cast unbelieving glances at Entreri. He shrugged. "It isn't really the treasury, but the gift room beside the treasury. And it isn't really a fire, but a certain present from Neverwinter, one that emits a sleep-inducing smoke. The guards will rush to the treasury only to lie down and nap."

A murmur of mirth passed among the crew as they listened to the growing sounds of mayhem. The shouts and stamping feet died away to silence.

"Follow me. Swords out."

They did, their steps confident behind their ingenious leader. He had thought of everything.

Noph reached his free hand toward Shar, but she moved away, approaching Entreri. Her own free hand grasped the assassin's, and his fingers squeezed.

Congratulations, Entreri, you damned skunk, Noph thought.

Behind him, Ingrar tripped on a chair leg. Noph glanced back at the blind young man: he looked white-faced and shaky.

"Let me guide you along," Noph suggested, hand grasping his.

Ingrar nodded and gripped Noph's hand tightly.

"Bring him up here," Entreri hissed. He and Shar stood at the two grand double doors—white, with gold leaf on a filigree trim.

"The master summons," Noph told Ingrar, though the blind man was already hurrying toward the voice. In a panting moment more, the two reached the double doors.

"Give it a sniff," Entreri said. "Is anybody out there?"

Ingrar drew a deep breath through the door space.

Conflicting emotions crossed his face. At last, he released the air in a whisper. "One guard remaining. He's young. He's standing against the wall to the right side."

"Good enough for me," Entreri said noncommittally, kicking the right door outward.

Wood and iron thumped against a soft bulk. It groaned once and slid. A young guard slumped from behind the door. His face was ringed with the downy curls of an early beard.

Entreri glanced at the blind man. "You couldn't smell the beard?"

Without further comment, he and Shar shoved past the half-open door and the unconscious guard and stalked down the curving hallway. A wave of Shar's hand hastened Noph and Ingrar forward.

"Anyone up here?" Entreri asked.

Panting as he and Noph caught up, Ingrar replied, "Used to be. The smell is cold, stale. They're gone. Wait. There's one at the head of the audience chamber. On the right. Just ahead, around the bend."

"Young? A beard?" teased Shar.

Ingrar shrugged. "I'd say, yes."

Entreri drew a dagger from his belt and skulked forward. "Lucky for him you did." He slightly modified his grip on the dagger before hurling it.

The blade flashed through the air, slipped past the white belly of the wall, and struck the young guard in the head. He convulsed once before collapsing, bloodless, to the ground.

"Excellent aim," Shar commented.

"I didn't have to hit him with the handle, you know," Entreri said coldly. "Noph, keep the Seer close at hand."

Following the assassin's lead, the pirates dashed to the gilded double doors of the audience chamber. Entreri shoved the unconscious man out of the way, retrieved his dagger, and threw back the doors. Cold, humid air rolled over the group.

Ingrar gasped a breath. "Not in there, Master Entreri. Not in there. We're not going in there."

"What? What is it?"

"Death," said Ingrar. "Our deaths. All of our deaths. The deaths of every creature on this cursed coast."

Entreri looked at the rest of his party, their faces white and wary. "See? I told you the bloodforge was in here," he said flatly. With that, the assassin strode into the audience chamber of King Aetheric III.

Noph tugged a reluctant Ingrar. "Let's go. We've signed on this far." Stepping past the fallen guard, they entered the chamber.

\* \* \* \* \*

*We should have heeded their presence. We should have known this assassin could slay even us. But with fiends flooding the city, bloodforge armies appearing against them, and the smell of death so strong in our gills . . . with the apocalypse descending around us, Artemis Entreri and his band were no more than cuttlefish splashing in tidal pools.*

*We should have known they could slay even us. But we could not have stopped them, anyway—not and fought the fiends.*

\* \* \* \* \*

The audience chamber of the mage-king was dank, cavernous, and black. The air was heavy. At the far end of the lightless chamber hung thick ebony curtains. The empty darkness in front of the drapes seemed to be swimming with phantasms—tiny crayfish and sea sprites and spineless creatures floating in air. A deep, quiet rumble filled the chamber, and minute water sounds—eddies, waves, vague liquid voices. . . .

Entreri wasted no time. He rushed with Shar to the

curtain and drew back one small edge of it to reveal a triangle of thick glass beyond. He stuck his silvered plate to the glass.

Within the tank, something enormous stirred. It moved with silent, slippery ease. A broad circle of deeper darkness appeared at the top of the triangle of glass. It descended within the tank and hovered beside the curtain's edge.

"What is it?" Shar asked, gazing at the circle of night.

Digging in one of his many pockets, the assassin said, "It doesn't matter. The mage-king can't reach through. His poison can't come through. I placed the portal, and I command it."

"It's an eye," Shar whispered in realization. She stared at the huge spot. "That's what it is. A wide-open eye."

Noph led a trembling Ingrar up beside them. "I hope you've got something superterrific up your sleeve, boss."

Entreri nodded. He extended a clenched hand, and then opened his fingers to reveal a palmful of white pills. "One's enough to purify a lake. Twenty-five will make this tank taste like a mountain spring."

The others looked confused.

The assassin tossed the handful of pills into the silver plate. They soundlessly disappeared into it. On the far side of the thick glass, the white tablets emerged and slowly sank, bubbling, toward the unseeable bottom.

Entreri turned, took Shar's hand, and said, "Let's go."

"That's it?" Rings asked as he and the others dogged the assassin's heels.

Entreri herded them toward the double doors. "We'll probably want to be a good distance away when the mage-king shatters his tank."

"Shatters his tank?" Noph echoed.

"From what you've told us, he needs salt water and the poisons of his own skin to survive. What sustains him would kill us, and vice versa. What do you think pure water will do to him? It'll burn like acid. It'll make him break out. It'll leave the bloodforge undefended."

Another voice spoke, a deep, wounded, angry voice.

*"Why have you done this? Why?"*

The mage-king.

Entreri didn't answer. He headed with a little more speed toward the doorway.

The voice grew louder. Sounds of boiling came from the tank.

*"We keep the fiends at bay. Kill us, and you kill yourselves, you kill this whole land."*

As the pirates passed through the double doors, Entreri muttered calmly, "The water is completely pure by now."

The mage-king roared:

*"You, Artemis Entreri, you and yours, are our eternal enemies! You have slain us, and all of Doegan!"*

"Head for high ground," the assassin quietly advised.

\* \* \* \* \*

Trandon raised his staff to receive the next fiend. But it was not merely one: a whole wall of the villains rushed toward him. A retreat? Still, by sheer force of numbers, they would sweep all the defenders under.

"Brace for it!" shouted Trandon to his companions.

The others looked, and chorused a groan. One by one, they finished off their current adversaries and braced for the new onslaught.

Trandon stood, staff lifted high to crack the first head that came. "It has been an honor to battle beside you three!"

"Aye!" came Jacob's reply through bloody teeth.

"Let the bards sing Tyr's praises!" Kern added.

"Aye!" joined Miltiades.

The demon tidal wave crested as it approached. Fiends tumbled over each other, trampling comrades in their haste. There came a moment of shrieks and blood and flailing.

Trandon split one head with the tip of his staff and another with the butt; Jacob's sword hewed the back of a skeletal warrior; Kern pounded the bleating foes into messy piles of flesh and bone; and Miltiades stood above them all, eyes gleaming with righteous fury as his hammer slew four, five, six fiends.

The wave swept onward.

Behind that sanguine line of fleeing fiends came another wave, mightier than the first.

Black-armored warriors.

Black-robed war wizards.

The conjured defenders of Doegan.

They advanced relentlessly, chopping into the backs of the fleeing monsters. This line, too, passed the wounded paladins, leaving them to stand and gape after the retreating battle.

"What was that?" Kern wondered aloud.

Miltiades's voice was a growl of condemnation. "A bloodforge army, no doubt. Wicked defenders of a wicked regime."

"Still," Jacob said, patting the dust from his clothes, "they saved us from the fiends."

Miltiades nodded grimly. "You need healing, Kern."

The golden warrior looked at his shoulder. "I suppose I do."

Miltiades drew a deep breath, closed his eyes, placed his hands on the wound, and offered a silent prayer to Tyr. Even as the holy power moved through him, stitching together sinews and muscles and mending cracked bones, Kern glanced at Jacob.

"I was sure at one point I saw you stuck on the end of a trident," the golden paladin said.

Jacob blinked back at him and shook his head. "Not me." He gestured at his clothes, dusty but bloodless. "Maybe it was Trandon."

As Miltiades lifted his hands from the healed shoulder of his comrade, Kern said, "Was it you, then, Trandon?" They turned to see the tall warrior gazing down at his chest.

Trandon's voice was hesitant, filled with awe. "No blood, here, but something else." The pendant glowed brilliantly. "Eidola is here. She is nearby."

Kern's eyes grew wide. "My antimagic must have worn off!"

"Or perhaps the warding magic around Eidola was compromised when the fiends attacked," Trandon offered.

"Conjuring that army must have taken its toll," Miltiades said. "The mage-king must have diverted power from cloaking his captive."

"Are you saying—?" Kern began.

"The only way to find out is to head for the palace, and watch the pendant," Miltiades said.

Trandon was already rushing up the road toward the abode of the mage-king.

Though the four paladins ran for the palace, they could not outrun the descending night. Deep darkness had fallen by the time they reached the stair bridge in front of the palace. They paused, panting, and gazed out over the city.

The distant thunder of battle filled the air. From this high vantage, the warriors could make out the line of defenders, holding fast in most places. Fire and smoke rose in a thick curtain around the city.

"There," Miltiades said, pointing to a spot a mere quarter mile distant. "They've broken through." The others then saw it, a company of fiends charging past a quickly closing breech. "They'll be here in mere moments."

"But the pendant is nearly blinding, now," Kern said, holding hands up before his face. "She must be here, in the palace. We must proceed."

Miltiades's face was a mask of soot and scars. "I would, but for those fiends. They are after one thing—the bloodforge. For the good of all Toril, we cannot let them have it." He unslung his warhammer and marched grimly up the steps of the stair bridge. "The only way for land-bound creatures to cross the moat is to climb here." He reached a small landing just ahead of the palace facade. "We hold them here, as long as we can. The fiends will pay a dear toll in blood to pass."

Kern marched up beside him, hammer flashing. "I will take the vanguard and draw them in, slaying with my antimagic."

Trandon said, "I will be at your one hand, and Jacob at your other. No claw will touch you."

Even as they arrayed themselves and kicked footholds, the fiends converged on the stairway and charged upward.

In moments, the villainous horde crashed against them. Kern and Miltiades flung them back with killing blows, alternating like a pair of men driving stakes into the ground. Jacob hacked and hewed. Trandon hurled attackers into the moat. Shorn claws and cracked skulls tumbled bloodily down to stick on the spikes below. The defenders held.

The fiends bunched up along the stairs and began slaying each other to get by. Those that could fly took to the air, but other defenders in the palace beyond sent whispering shafts into them. They dropped among the other dead in the moat.

In the air or on the stair, the fight was furious. Some fiends were unmade by the convulsing limbs and acidic blood of their slain comrades. Others merely crowded themselves from the causeway and dropped onto impaling spikes. But many, if not most, fell to the powerful blows of the paladins.

"We are holding them," Miltiades grunted as his warhammer pulped the pod-shaped head of a greater fiend. "We are holding back the armies of hell!"

Then one fiend slipped past—a great anaconda with the head of a boar. Miltiades pounded its slithering side, but couldn't stop it. A second got by, and a third. In time, the tide of fiends flowed once more. For the defenders, all that remained was the grim, bloody work of slaying those they could.

Miltiades shouted, "May Tyr bless the palace defenders!"

## Chapter 8
## *Confluence*

As the pirates fled into the hall, Noph glanced back toward the audience chamber.

The twin curtains of the mage-king's tank drew slowly aside to reveal a tank glowing with fiery radiance. Orange-red water churned and boiled around a thrashing, titanic creature. Mangled, scaly, tentacular—the mage-king writhed: his torso arched in agony; his tentacles spasmed; his hands clutched into fists; his teeth ground together like rolling boulders. Aetheric thrashed, recoiled, shuddered, but all the while held those tank-bursting fists by his sides. His skin molted away. It sloughed in ribbons in the water. It circled him in tatters. Still, he did not break the glass.

A sniff and a tug from Ingrar brought Noph back around. "We've got more problems. Brimstone—there are fiends ahead. Tanar'ri. They're pouring up the stairs in front of the palace."

"Swords! Knives!" Noph called to his comrades. "Fiends ahead."

"Damn," Belgin swore. He came to a halt and drew steel. "Why don't we escape down a side passage—let the fiends and the mage-king take care of each other?"

Entreri shook his head. "And let demons have first crack at the bloodforge? No. We stand and fight."

Noph helped Ingrar to the side of the hall. "You wait here. I'll keep anybody from coming at you." He drew his sword.

"Sure," Ingrar responded, hefting his cutlass. "Just don't back up into me; I'll stab anything that comes close."

There was time for nothing more. Shattering glass and splintering wood announced the army's arrival. Fiends smashed through the front facade of the palace and flooded toward the pirates.

Entreri and his party stood unmoving, a circle of swords against an army of fangs. The onslaught came, unstoppable.

Noph set his stance and prepared to die.

Then another, deeper shattering came. The fist of the mage-king smashed the impenetrable wall of his tank. Water blasted through the breach, and cracks ran out from it in all directions. The glass held for one final moment before it all—glass, water, and squid-lord— roared out and struck the opposite wall of the audience chamber.

The wall creaked, then gave way. Ten-ton stone blocks fragmented into flying rubble and scouring sand. Rock sprayed outward. In its midst came one of the king's tentacles, as wide around as an elephant.

"Down!" Noph shouted. He and Ingrar dropped to their faces.

The others did, too. A killing hail of stone, sand, and water roared by overhead. It rushed straight into the teeth of the charging tanar'ri, ripping flesh from bone.

Noph saw no more. The flood arrived.

A muscular wave hoisted him from the floor and tossed him in its black belly. The breath he held blasted from his lungs. He tried to swim, but the water was omnipotent.

A great wall of tentacle swept beneath him. His cheek scraped the bossed ceiling. A chandelier surged by. Then he saw it again, that great black circle, that deep, deep darkness.

The eye of Aetheric.

Noph kicked out away from the mage-king's face and dropped into a small side eddy.

He plunged. Down, down. Whirlpool. It emptied water through a doorway and down. It emptied him. Water rushed in a choppy cascade down, down, down. Tumble tumble turn, down. Spiral stairs cracked his knees. Torches glowed lurid before they snuffed, and down, down.

The stair went black. Chaos. Blunt blows. Panicked roar.

And down.

\* \* \* \* \*

A great roar came from behind the paladins, from the very palace of the mage-king. The battle stilled for a moment as every eye lifted skyward. Stars were suddenly falling from the heavens. Huge chunks of firmament whistled down in a terrific rain.

"The Day of Tyr," gasped Miltiades, breathless. "The end of time. The Coming of Justice." Suddenly oblivious to the foes before him, he dropped to one knee.

The other paladins did likewise. Their heads bowed down just as a massive boulder of masoned stone bounced over them and struck the gaping fiends below. The rock splattered the first few beasts. Then it rolled down the stairs, grinding demons to grist.

"Do you see?" Miltiades cried, elated. " 'And my hammer shall smite the nations of darkness and grind them into bitter meal.' "

The bowed heads lifted, just in time for them all to witness the next onslaught. A massive flood vaulted over them. It bore in its churning belly the twisted, broken bodies of more fiends. They soared by overhead in a cascade of blood and water.

" 'And I shall cast them down from on high, as the blacksmith casts down the burrs of iron that cling to his new-forged hammer. They shall fall from the heavens on this, my day, that all peoples of every land will know that the hammer of justice descends.' " As Miltiades spoke these words, a spray of water and blood swept over them. The bodies of fiends plunged down all around.

Kern cried out, "How could we have doubted you, Tyr? How could we have listened to the profanities of a tentacled beast instead of the precepts of justice?" He turned to the silver warrior. "There is no Fallen Temple. There is only the True Temple—only we, the faithful of Tyr! Let us rescue Eidola, and save Doegan!"

The ground trembled.

The skies split open.

The rain of fiends faltered and ceased.

The wheels of Tyr's chariot roared thunder.

Kern and Miltiades turned toward the sound, toward the coming of Tyr in glory. What they saw was not Tyr, though, but his enormous, bleeding apotheosis.

Aetheric III dragged himself up from the broken dome of his palace. His hands seized and smashed turrets. His tentacles coiled and recoiled in slug paths of steaming slime. His throat, so long filled with poison, roared.

*"Doegan, behold your god!"*

## Chapter 9

## Conspiracy

Noph awoke in the dark palace dungeon. He slouched against a wall of stone, water covering him to his chest. He could smell the sullen ash of doused torches, and could hear the gentle drip of wet ceilings. He saw little. The only light in the place sifted faintly down from the spiral stairs at either end of the corridor.

"Ingrar?" he muttered stupidly. His voice was raw. Coughing spastically, Noph spat out salty foam. "Is anyone else alive down here?"

A woman's voice came from a nearby cell. "Who's there? Who is it?"

More water rattled in Noph's lungs. "Who are you?"

"I am Eidola Neverwinter," said the woman.

Noph struggled to his feet. "I'm coming. I'm coming." He steadied himself on a wall, then lumbered along the flooded corridor. "I've got to find a key." He dragged the toe of his boot, searching for—

With a splash, he tripped atop a guard's body. Noph struggled to one side and felt for a ring of keys. Finding it, he ripped it free from the man's belt.

"I'm coming. I'm coming."

Noph reached the cell door where he had heard the voice and started fitting key after key into the slot. His hands jangled excitedly.

The lady is within. I will rescue her, he thought. Another voice stirred in the back of his mind. What if Entreri is right? What if she is an agent of the Unseen? What if she is a monster?

A key clicked. The cell door swung open. Noph gulped and stepped into the breach. With an effort he quashed his doubts. Surely the paladins were right. Surely Khelben would not have given them this commission if he'd had any doubts of Eidola's bona fides.

In the deep darkness, he could see little. Then he felt a warm wave of relief wash over him. On the far wall, he made out a feminine outline—long hair plastered to thin shoulders, a curve of hips, lean but strong legs. The woman's arms were held out to either side by massive shackles bolted into the wall, and her legs, submerged in the fetid flow of Aetheric's shattered tank, were bound together by a broad band of iron.

"I'm Kastonoph Nesher," Noph said stupidly. To make matters worse, he realized he was bowing. "Your husb—your groo—Piergeiron sent me."

"Thank the gods," the lady replied. Her voice was as raw as his. "Get me loose!"

"Right," Noph said, glad she had given him a bit of direction. He stepped forward, keys jingling in his hand. "You wouldn't know which of these keys—"

"Just hurry," the lady implored.

"Right," Noph replied again. He edged up to her, selected a key, felt the bond on her right arm until he located the slot, and tried it. No good. The key was too large. He tried the next. It slid in, but didn't engage the lock.

"Kastonoph?" she said.

"Yes?" he replied, startled.

"I was just trying to remember your name."

"My friends call me Noph." He continued with the keys. "Ah, got the first one!" He flung back the shackle.

Eidola's arm dropped loosely free. She let out a hiss of pain. "Lift it! Lift it!"

"Lift what?"

"My arm! Now!"

Noph fumbled in the dark. His hand brushed the lady's side, smooth and warm in the harsh coldness. He found her arm and raised it.

"Ah, that's better," she gasped out. "I've been this way for days. We'll have to ease them down slowly. In the meantime, try the same key on the other lock."

"Yes, milady." Still holding her free arm up, Noph stretched across her body to the other shackle. He couldn't quiet reach.

"This is a dungeon, not a boudoir. Touch me if you have to!"

Noph drew a deep breath and leaned against her. The key slid into the shaft—thank Tyr, and the lock clicked. Noph hurriedly flipped open the shackle.

"Up! Up! Lift it!" she growled as her left arm fell.

Noph caught the limb and lifted it. "There—how's that?"

"Better," she whispered, panting.

"Um, Lady Eidola, I'm going to need to lower your arms to get your legs free."

He could sense her jaw clenching. "All right. Slowly—*slowly*—lower my arms to rest on your shoulders."

Noph nodded. He felt himself blush. What would Piergeiron say to see his young protege pressed against his bride like this, lowering her arms into an embrace? Noph took a step back and drew the lady's arms inward and down. She groaned and arched against him, her limbs trembling. At last, her arms rested on his shoulders.

"All right. That wasn't so bad," the lady sighed. "Now, just as slowly, kneel down to open the shackle on my legs."

"Yes."

Stiffly, Noph slid down into the cold, black waters. Eidola's arms dragged along his descending shoulders, and she moaned. The flood lapped at her knees. He could see her wavering reflection in the water, caught and shattered by ripples and waves into a thousand Eidolas. Noph settled beside her feet and allowed himself a huff of air.

Get hold of yourself, he thought. What's wrong with you?

The cold felt good on his feverish body. He reached beneath the chill surface, ran his hand from her delicate feet to her ankle and onto the first gentle rise of her calf. The stout iron casement was just above. Still clutching the key that had released her hands, he found the slot and slid the metal rod gently in. A click answered the turn of the key, and the iron shackle swung open.

"You're free!" he said.

Clutching his head now, Eidola tried to step from the wall. Something at her midsection tugged. "Damn. That's right. There's one more restraint—this wretched chastity belt."

"Chastity belt?" Noph sputtered. "Of all the barbaric—Surely Piergeiron hadn't fitted you with—"

"No, not him. My captors. What good is a kidnapped virgin unless she remains one?"

"B-But why do you want m-me to remove your ch-ch-chas-?"

"Calm down," Eidola replied. "It's enspelled to keep me from running away, from disobeying my captors. The buckles are in back."

Dutifully, Noph rose from the black flood. His clothes clung uncomfortably against him.

"Hurry up!" Eidola begged.

Noph reached around the lady's warm, smooth hips and just inside her outer shift. He gently felt along her spine for the buckles of her belt.

"Your fingers are cold," she said.

"I'm trying to hurry," Noph replied.

He found the buckles and breathed a nervous sigh. Numb fingers worked at the leather. The first strap popped loose, flinging up a fingerful of water. Noph startled, almost hollering. As he fiddled with the next two buckles, he tried to make conversation. "You know, I used to be a paladin. Now I'm a pirate."

Eidola's voice was chilly. "Why would a pirate want to rescue me?"

"Oh, the others don't. They want to kill you. They think you're an agent of the Unseen."

"And what if I am?"

His cold fingers paused, the last buckle of the belt halfway undone.

The golden lasso, he thought. The lasso of truth. It will show what you really are.

A splash came in the hall, interrupting his thoughts. Then another splash, and another.

"Hurry," she whispered. "It's Lord Garkim!"

Noph drew his hand away from her hips and reached for the lasso. He undid the catch and felt the loops drop into his hand.

"Hurry!" she breathed.

He slipped the lasso over her head . . . and everything changed.

Lady Eidola was gone.

In her place was a scale-skinned gray beast with large, empty eyes.

A greater doppleganger.

Next moment, she was a convulsing crocodile.

The monster's scaly midsection burst the final buckle, and the crocodile fell on Noph. Its teeth flashed in the darkness and fastened on his chest. With a terrific splash, it dragged him down beneath the icy murk.

## *Interlude*

# Condemnation

I'm mesmerized by your warm, warm flesh, cold monstrosity beneath.

You're the third lady . . . there was Aleena Paladin-star she is spirit, an angel hello, Aleena . . . there was Sharessa No-Angel a creature of flesh carnal . . . there is you, infernal woman demonspawn.

You're all the same; I'm mesmerized by you . . . powerful, elegant, mysterious, unattainable . . . all the same.

You can't be held . . . no man, not even a kidnapper, can hold you . . . can't be held . . . no fingers, no claws, nothing in all of creation not even a golden, unerring lasso . . . you can't be held . . . I can't hold you . . . are killing me for trying . . . your teeth meet between my ribs . . . hello, Teeth.

You hear something . . . where are those nice warm teeth now where is your muscle-back . . . I drift in cold ink . . . you are done with me you held me and are done . . . I am dead already.

I have not climbed the stormy tops . . . I have not slain a dozen foes . . . I have not slain even you . . . maybe they will still shoehorn me into the dinghy and toss the comet-torch to flare up and say there goes another piece of the great pirate Blackfingers Ralingor . . . because after all I've now had just about everything that was soft in me torn away.

## Chapter 10

## Divergence

*We heard and saw it all.*

*We did not hear it with our own ears, bleeding above our ruined palace as we crushed fiends in our tentacles.*

*We did not see it with our own eyes, reaching where our flesh could not to slay with spell and thought among the teeming demons.*

*We heard and saw it with our lower mind, our animal mind. We knew it not so much by sound and sight but by smell, knew the goodness and badness of it.*

*This was how the destroyers of Doegan met again.*

Their second convergence was in every way the opposite of their first. They met not in a morning-bright plaza, but in a night-dark dungeon. Only Trandon's pendant lit the way for the paladins, and for the pirates only makeshift torches, casting a feverish glow across the groin vaults. The two groups did not arrive slowly, either, one party on either side of a pristine fountain; they spilled into the dungeon from opposite staircases, glimpsed each other and rushed together. They met and fought before an open cell door, their hammers and cutlasses crashing against each other to prevent entry to their foes. And on either side of the fray the groups were minus a man. The paladins had lost the young convert Noph, and the pirates had lost the old veteran, Anvil.

The only thing that had remained the same was that both sides still sought the Lady Eidola, one for rescue and the other for murder.

Great Miltiades, champion of virtue, battled haft to hilt with agile Entreri, champion of vice. Sword and warhammer clashed against one another, sending showers of sparks hissing into the water that rose to their knees.

"Give way, Entreri," snarled Miltiades. "You will not prevail here. You shall have to slay every last one of us before you lay a hand upon Lady Eidola."

"If you insist," Entreri returned, jabbing inward with his sword and nicking the great warrior's neck.

Miltiades answered the attack with a thunderous blow to the assassin's chest, driving him back.

Their seconds, Shar and Kern, fought beside them.

Shar's blade and wit were as sharp as ever. "Well, Kern, from the moment we met, you've been trying to get me to a dark, secluded spot. I'm glad you brought your love hammer."

Kern's response came with a swing of his mighty maul. "If I had my way, Lady, I'd have rescued you from the darkness. It is you who are devoted to dirt and dank."

"Whether we do it dirty or clean, we're still doing it!"

The others—Jacob and Trandon on one side, and Rings, Belgin, and Ingrar on the other—were shut out of the fight. They stood at the ready in knee-deep water.

Steel rang on silver, iron on gold. Swords carved crescents of shadow into the crumbling walls of stone. Hammers flung up jeweled spray.

In the midst of this graceful deadliness came an ungainly sound—a half-drowned shout, a clumsy splash, and the sharp slap of something muscular diving beneath the waves.

Hammer and sword faltered for a moment. In the tangled web of light from talisman and torches, the foes saw something black and swift dart into the watery space between them. It trailed a golden cord.

Miltiades and Entreri more than glimpsed the scaly bulk of the crocodile; they felt it. The creature lashed Entreri's feet from under him, and the assassin sprawled backward into the muck; it rammed Miltiades's legs, and he fell. Paladin and pirate landed side by side and sat up to see the black monster shoot through the water to the base of the stairs.

In the blink of an eye, the scaly beast transformed into a black-furred mastiff with a golden leash. It bounded up the stairs and out of sight.

A gurgling shout came again from the cell, "That's her! Eidola! The doppleganger!"

Trandon splashed to the cell door. The glaring jewel showed a bloody young man leaning against the far wall. "It's Noph!" Even as he said it, the jewel on his neck began to fade. He glanced at the dark stairway. "She's getting away!"

Miltiades rose, magnificent in his streaming armor. His face was a fiery red in the torchlight. "How can it be? That was not Eidola!"

Trandon responded, "Look at this fading jewel. Who else could it be?"

Miltiades grew furious in the dawning realization. "For this we have come? To rescue a monster? Follow me, any who wish to do justice on that creature's head!" He shouldered his hammer and charged down the hall, uncaring whether anyone followed.

Jacob was just steps behind the mighty paladin.

Kern glanced after his comrades, sloshed to the cell, and looked in at Noph. His face was grave. "That boy will need a paladin's touch if he is to live."

Trandon, beside him, clapped him on the shoulder. "Let's get to it, before the jewel goes out completely." They entered the watery cell.

Entreri narrowly watched the paladin's company divide. Half rushed off to slay the creature they had come to rescue. The other half remained to—to *what?* To save a companion they had rejected? Or did they have something else in mind, perhaps the acquisition of a great, arcane artifact?

The bloodforge.

In a low growl, Entreri said, "Rings, Belgin, go after the doppleganger. Join the damned paladins if you must, but make sure one of you slays her. We want our reward."

The dwarf and the sharper looked dubiously at their employer. Rings's nostrils flared. "What are the rest of you going to do?"

"We've a companion to aid—" his voice dropped to a hiss "—and an even greater treasure to secure. Now, get gone!"

It was as quick as that. The archenemies that had converged moments before diverged again, now as allies. Miltiades, Jacob, Rings, and Belgin would pursue the doppleganger to the end of Faerûn, if need be, and slay her. Meanwhile, Entreri, Shar, Ingrar, Trandon, and Kern would minister to Noph and seek the unspoken cause of all this folly—the bloodforge of Doegan.

As Rings and Belgin rushed up the stairs after their

quarry, Kern and Trandon knelt within the cell and laid hands on Noph. The boy had been ripped to shreds. His chest was a mass of holes.

Still in the corridor, Entreri took the blind man by the arm and ushered him toward the dungeon cell.

"Why me, Master Entreri?" asked Ingrar. "Why did you choose to have me along?"

The assassin replied coldly. "We've a palace of wreckage to sniff through. The bloodforge is there."

*It was, indeed. But we were there, too. And we would defend the bloodforge with our very life.*

## Epilogue
# Confederates

I'm mesmerized by you.

By all of you.

There you are, Kern, golden-haired with eyes of blue skies. Holy. Your hands bring healing fire into the tattered remnants of my chest. Your fingers lace together ribbons of flesh. Your faith binds tooth holes, each one large enough that, if you wanted, you could reach in and tickle my heart.

And, then, there is you, Master Entreri, my rival. If I die, it will be your back that carries me out of this ruin. You will hide me away until I can be placed in the sea.

You will light the torch that burns away my boat, my body, that falls on me like a dying star.

And what of you, Sharessa, the Shadow, the shapely Sharker? You're a promising stream, full of life, that sinks and dies in desert sands.

And Trandon, there you stand. The once-bright gem you wear fades. It is as if what you once believed in is slowly abandoning you. I know how you feel. And yet, still, you stand there. Is that what it is to be grown up? To embrace not faith but doubt, and still stand?

And you, Ingrar—the Seer. If I live, you will teach me to gain in what I have lost, as you have gained new eyes for old. Eyes that see past double walkers and doppelgangers to the truth beyond.

And finally you, Mage-King Aetheric III—you, who have risen above your palace and your poison to become more than you were.

Let me, likewise, rise with thee.

### The story continues...

### The DOUBLE DIAMOND TRIANGLE SAGA™

The bride of the Open Lord of Waterdeep has been abducted. The kidnappers are from the far-off lands of the Utter East. But who are they? And what do they really want? Now a group of brave paladins must travel to the perilous kingdoms of this unknown land to find the answers. But in this mysterious world, nothing is ever quite what it appears.

### Look for the books in the series

*The Abduction*
(January 1998)

*The Paladins*
(January 1998)

*The Mercenaries*
(January 1998)

*Errand of Mercy*
(February 1998)

*An Opportunity for Profit*
(March 1998)

*Conspiracy*
(April 1998)

*Uneasy Alliances*
(May 1998)

*Easy Betrayals*
(June 1998)

*The Diamond*
(July 1998)

### Coming in May

### UNEASY ALLIANCES
By David Cook with Peter Archer

Paladins and mercenaries have joined forces to defeat an attacking army of fiends. Now a powerful new weapon, the bloodforge, comes into their hands. But some suspect that their leader's plans for the weapon are less than honorable. Can they undermine his hidden motives, while holding off the fiendish army?

### Coming in June

### EASY BETRAYALS
By Richard Baker

A mixed company of paladins and mercenaries race back to Faerûn after the object of their quest is revealed as a threat to peace and order through the Realms. But beware! the evil will lead them on a chase that ends in the last place any of them expected.

### Coming in July

### THE DIAMOND
By J. Robert King & Ed Greenwood

The quest has taken two parties across the Realms. Now the heroes gather at Waterdeep, where it all began, for a final celebration. But there are still a few loose ends to tie up. . . .